REDEEM
THE KNIGHT

REDEEM THE KNIGHT

By David V. Mammina

A Dark Fantasy Novel

Published by David V. Mammina
Printed by Lulu

REDEEM THE KNIGHT

By David V. Mammina

978-0-615-48134-0
Copyright © 2011 by David V. Mammina
Printed by Lulu, Inc. All rights reserved.
Printed in the United States of America
Cover illustration by Hugo Bravo
www.bravoillustrations.com

Due to the dynamic nature of the internet, some of these websites may not still be active and others may have been established after the publication of this book and, therefore, are not listed.
www.MamminaBooks.com
www.lulu.com/mammina

Dedicated to those who believe in the following phrase:

"Redemption, through God, is promised."

Other works by DVM:

The Angels of Resistance
Parts I & II
(2005, 2007, 2009*)

Protector of Children:
Assassin's Dreams
(2008)

Paltronis
(2010)

*2009 is the combined updated version of the two books.

Author's Note

First, I would like to thank you for picking up this new title. I am very proud of it and believe that it will inspire you. What I have written here, essentially, is a natural prequel to *The Angels of Resistance*, taking place about four hundred years or so before. Now, don't worry. If you did not read that book, your experience with this one will not change whatsoever. It stands on its own.

Secondly, if I may, it is necessary to clarify a term that is used freely by some and not truly understood by most. I have used the paladins as a major aspect of the story, until it hit me. Not many know what a paladin is! So, here is a brief drop of knowledge for those that do not know. A paladin is a holy officer associated with the old virtues of the Holy Roman Empire and the Catholic Church. Notice its use in a poem I wrote for you. I hope you enjoy the story as much as I have enjoyed writing it. Many thanks and God bless.

Rise of the Paladins

In a world marred by greed and lust,
comes a renewed army of the just.
When there was no peace or rest,
the forsaken put them to the test.

A holy order from long ago,
a fortified legion to defeat any foe.
May God smile upon the righteous hand,
that buries the wicked in the sand.

At last, the true may have their day.
At last, the noble may have their say.
Let the paladins rise and have their start,
from mace to shield and cross to heart.

A

Redeem the Knight
Prologue

Excerpt from the Paladin's Compendium

13. This is how the world as they knew it came to an end. As it were, human civilization was nearly at its peak, though their worst enemies were the kind they could not defeat outright. Aside from natural disasters, disease was adapting to their advanced treatments. Nevertheless, their greed, violence, and faithlessness brought true calamity upon them.

14. While they fought incessant wars over a secret cure for deadly malignances, fire rained down from the sky. They tried to destroy it with their sophisticated weaponry, but the meteor blasted into cataclysmic debris and fell upon the earth for three days and two nights. If humankind had not suffered enough from the scourge of war, millions more fell under the might of the deadly shower.

15. Several power stations holding lethal energy were obliterated, expelling tons of toxins into the atmosphere. Untainted food and water were scarce. The air was awful to breath. In time, only the coasts of the Great Pacifica sustained life. This was the beginning of the end for them.

16. Ironically, their great civilization obtained a sense of pride over the previous centuries and became self-dependent. Their inventions were made for war and indulgence. This convenient way of advancing did not follow the way of God. They made nothing to last. Digital devices, rather than stone or even paper, recorded their history.

17. Without power or electricity, their entire foundation of existence had been devastated. While some survived, most were unable to thrive in the new world. Basic instincts set in, for only the strongest survived. The once superior civilization that forgot where they had come from turned primal.

18. Now, centuries later, God's people have risen to new heights. They have, essentially, returned to their feudal roots and established new civilizations about the limited inhabitable land. With this new height, came a new meaning. Some have been chosen to lead this new mission of survival, hope, and unity. Few have acquired such great powers from the Lord as the Paladins.

19. God created the paladins to heal and defend His people. They are of holy blood, born to join the ranks of others who answer to the Lord's calling. They are soldiers of God,

meant to relight the path of humanity. Disbelievers will say that the effects of the toxins and impurities of the old world mixed with the rise of newer races of people caused this phenomenon. Do not listen to such madness.

20. As God gave rise to paladins, the new world has also procured a new breed of humankind. For those who speak Christian, they call them "sorcerers." Sorcerers use their remarkable powers to bend the elements and laws of nature. While they are not deemed as evil, some use their powers for means of fear and conquest. This is why God blessed the new world with the paladin.

21. Paladins are resistant to most sorcerers and their powers. It is their charge to defend God's people from these wicked magicians. This is the Lord's counteraction to the transfiguration of sorcerers. Like the new sky bursting with stars, the new world shall prosper in remembrance of the Primeval Tragedy with paladins leading the way.

-Primeval Tragedy, 1:13-21

Get Ready

Redeem the Knight
Redemption I

Three years ago…

Of all the skills and talents that man has developed over the spans of his existence, there is only one for which he has mastered. Like a buried niche in the soul, he possesses the urge to engage in violence. No matter how sacred and no matter how naïve he may seem, the primal instincts linger still.

Here in the Paladin's Sanctum, Arl Baelin must answer for this natural sin. A paladin of once great honor and respect, Baelin entered the hall and stood within the center of the holy circle, awaiting his trial. He was not one of the more famous paladins of the New Vatican, but he would soon become the most infamous. His crimes resonated all throughout the Ellium Empire.

There had never been more spectators present for a paladin's trial before, as the craving to hear Baelin's dark tale proved too succulent for anyone to ignore. The seven high magistrates sat in their places just outside of the circle, governing the somber tone of the hall. Gorged with holy knights of various ranks, the sanctum served as a place of worship and a place of judgment. Today's convergence was of judgment alone.

Once the main doors to the hall clanked shut, the hall surrendered to an eerie hush and the magistrates began. Wasting little time, the elder peered away from Baelin's file and glared forward, proclaiming, "We, the High Magistrates of the Paladin's Sanctum, have read through your file, Sir Baelin, and it disturbs us, indeed. Might you know why that is?"

The paladin said nothing, robed in black and bound in chains. His pain was far too deep to care about his superiors' disturbances, for he experienced the horror within those files. He watched as they scrutinized him on paper, and then, in his silence. Baelin's brown wisps of hair cascaded down his unshaven face, barely concealing his torment.

"You were building quite a reputation in Islandia for being a true paladin." The magistrate proceeded from his seat, "On an island that needed God's grace evermore, you were their pillar of light. Now, you have cast a shadow over that land – over all of us in the process. It saddens us to see such a promising servant of God fall so far so fast. You dishonor our holy mission."

The magistrate's poisoning words were bellowing in his mind, driving him mad. He had endured enough from his enemies only to be stoned by his brothers-in-arms. Was all his service for nothing? As a paladin, Baelin was on the verge of restoring peace to an island plagued by tribal violence. As a man, he had everything taken away from him and no one to console him. He was to be made an example of in order to refurbish the glory of the New Vatican. How he despised politics.

Breaking his silence, Arl Baelin gasped, "Enough!"

Another magistrate interceded, "Yes. You wish to speak now? Go on. What say you?"

Breathing heavily in order to compose himself, Baelin warily retorted, "Am I to be your scapegoat? Is that all I am now? You said that you have read that file. I do not believe you, for a true magistrate would see my blight."

"And what is this blight?" The elder asked as recorders scribed every word.

Outraged by the proceedings, Baelin replied, "The Blood Reapers uncovered the location my home – where my family finds refuge. In the night, they broke into my house as cowards do and took their vengeance on my wife and child. They thought they killed me. They were wrong and they were punished."

"I must stop you there, young man." Another magistrate came forward, "You enacted vengeance upon them, not punishment. Furthermore, you failed to mention that the woman who falsely married you and bore your child was a heretic, a mage of black magic!"

"You dare curse the names of my wife and child!" Baelin cried out in vehement anger.

Among the gasps and muffled comments about the hall, the elder scolded him, "You will not have this argument, paladin!"

"They raped and beat my wife unto death and — my boy!" He sobbed amidst his wrath, "They swung him about like a doll and — and they — they killed him. Those pigs killed my child!"

In the hopes of easing the hearts of the sanctum's spectators, a magistrate held up his hand and said in a modest tone, "We are not denying the awful murders of your wife and infant child, but your actions of cold blooded revenge that ensued in return was unbecoming of a paladin. You left a path of death and mutilation in your wake. There is even evidence of torture! This is not a soldier of God. This is not a holy knight's conduct!"

Composing himself, Baelin withstood another judge's edict, "You used the Divine Mace to bludgeon the alleged leader of this cult. This is blasphemous! Two of the slain were known to be mentally unstable. They, too, suffered from the 'might' of your mace. I am willing to believe that they were lured into this vile gang of mages and raiders, but these are the lambs that you must shepherd as paladin! Was killing them so necessary, boy?"

Taking time to answer clearly, the paladin said, "In dispatching them, no one else may suffer their revolting attacks. This is the language they understand."

"And what does that mean, paladin?" A magistrate said.

Shaking his head, Baelin exclaimed, "The Blood Reapers of Islandia received their name by drinking the blood of the opponents they kill. Mages of the black arts can draw power from your soul just the same. These people cannot be reasoned with. They do not want peace. They do not want prayers. They wish for only death. So, I gave it to them."

"Enough of this nonsense." The elder interceded, "Do you deny marrying a heretic, seeking vengeance for her and your son's murder, and slaying your victims in cold blood wielding the Divine Mace? What say you?"

Baelin wished to say many things in his irate and hurt spirit. Why prolong the cruelty of the trials? His cries would not be heard here in the place where he was instated as paladin seven years ago. His beloved wife, Gideon, and his innocent son, Alec, would not be avenged by way of his hissing. He killed the leader of the Blood Reapers and spared him no mercy. That was the vengeance of a fatherless man with no love left in his heart.

He looked up and said, "No. I deny nothing."

"Then, by the powers of the magistrates, you are guilty. With any—" The elder magistrate was interceded by another.

"Not all of the magistrates are finished with this trial, elder." One of them stood up and continued, "If found guilty, you will be stripped of your title and your crest and put in jail for two years. Then, you must redeem yourself. However, this would mean that the Divine Mace has deemed you unworthy to wield it any further. The paladin, as a holy knight living in an ungodly world, can sense and eliminate true evil—concentrated hatred and disdain for all things good and noble."

The elder returned the favor, "Will you tell us where you are leading the procession, Mason?"

Walking over to a lower knight holding a wooden square box, Magistrate Mason opened it and revealed Arl Baelin's Divine Mace. Among the reemerging gasps of the hall, Mason walked over to the fallen paladin and proclaimed, "As we all know, if the wielder of the mace can still call upon its divine power, the paladin still holds the very creeds of justice, charity, and purity in his heart. Perhaps, Baelin, if you still believe that you can serve God and His people here on this wretched earth, your mace will tell you so."

With everyone looking on, even the letting magistrates, Arl Baelin looked upon Magistrate Mason's good face and felt someone unchain his hands. Mason nodded and held the mace before him, permitting him to receive it. Feeling unworthy of its power, yet feeling remorseful even more, Baelin carefully took the mace into his right hand.

Now in Islandia, three years later…

In the west county of Seafare, two brave native soldiers have embarked on a special mission. In one of their hands, a private document written and stamped by the New Vatican revealed the location of Islandia's very own paladin. It was their revered duty to deliver the assignment straight to the holy knight himself. They did not mind the easy task, as it relieved them of their present obligations in the island's capital.

Bastian Spire, a stalwart veteran soldier and tracker, kept the documents safe in his pouch as he led the way for his younger companion and expert marksman, Ace Dolan. The paladin in their jurisdiction had the right to scour the region and seek out his own virtuous adventures, but this task required his full attention. Islandia sent out a plea to the New Vatican asking permission to utilize their paladin for a sensitive mission.

Nearing closer to their destination within the edges of the forest, they discussed the holy order in more detail. While scouting the area carefully, Bastian Spire proceeded, "And if the Divine Mace lit up in his hands, it was proof that it deemed him worthy to be a true paladin. Any true paladin can do this at will, you see."

"Okay?" Ace Dolan said, bewildered, "What happened when he took the mace? Did it light up?"

Confident that he was close now, Spire replied with his usual dapper grumbles, "They do not reveal those kinds of details outside of the sanctum. Nevertheless, he was banished here in this pleasant dump of an island to seek redemption, for this was where he lived and this was where he committed those 'dastardly' crimes."

"'Dastardly?' Please, he scrapped those cannibal psychos." Dolan countered, "If you ask me, he did us a service."

"I did not ask you." Spire grunted.

"And that matters, why?" Dolan grunted back.

Caught in a trance, the expert tracker raised his open hand and said steadily, "There it is. We are here."

They both stood on the edge of a sloping hill that led deeper into the forest, now able to make out what appeared to be the ruins of an ancient basilica. Taken by the veins and arteries of nature, the ruins seem to have deteriorated by time and dereliction. It hardly looked like the place for a holy knight to call home. Down the scrubby slope, a modest stream gently ran passed the site and disappeared into the dense woodlands.

"This?" Ace Dolan blustered, "This is where our illustrious paladin honestly —"

"Deal with it." Bastian Spire interrupted as he started down.

While murmuring, the gibing marksman followed the tracker down the hill. Birds resting within frantically flew out of the way and allowed the two soldiers to peruse the area. Dolan readied his short bow in the event that the paladin was not welcoming to unsolicited guests. After all, the New Vatican had not called upon the holy knight since his exile.

As exceptional as Bastian Spire was at spotting and disarming traps, he did not expect a trip wire near the ruins of the basilica. A graceless mistake, Spire felt the familiar tug upon his right foot and knew that he should not have let his guard down. From underneath loose foliage, a sturdy net had rushed upwards and snatched the two soldiers like fish from the sea. The counter weight log plummeted to the ground and consequently hoisted them up between two old trees.

Finding themselves in a sudden snare was only part of the problem. From the ruins below, a growling hound had ambled forth. Dolan had dropped his bow and Spire could hardly position himself to unsheathe his sword. The one dog was not the quandary. The real dilemma was who or what else it would attract to their vulnerable spot.

Before they could even attempt to escape the suspended entrapment, a man's voice emanated from somewhere close by, "Down boy."

He approached the obedient canine with a satchel of food and supplies around his shoulder. Sporting stubble, the stranger wore a grey cloak that lazily hung from his strapping frame. There were some distinct battle scars on the parts of his exposed body and each one with a story. His brown unruly hair seemed to accentuate his hazel eyes. Appearances aside, it was clear that he was the squatter of the basilica ruins.

"Down." The man caressed his friend's soft brown coat and surveyed his uninvited visitors above.

Bastian Spire held tightly to the mesh and grunted uncomfortably, "You are the paladin, Arl Baelin, I gather."

The man replied grimly, "Who are you and how did you find me?"

"Will you let us loose first?" Spire groaned.

The man gave his dog a meaty bone and let him run off before saying, "I am not in the business of repeating myself."

"I see. We are Islandic soldiers." He retorted and elongated his arm through the netting, presenting a significant satchel of his own, "And this pouch holds documents written and sealed by the New Vatican that will surely answer the rest of your questions."

Arl Baelin was never eager to trust the endearing promises of strangers. He, more than most people, knew how twisted and shrewd people could be. Yet, this news beckoned him like the moth to the flame. After bearing the longest three years of his life, Baelin felt as if his chance for redemption was at hand. Still skeptical, and rightfully so, the lone paladin dropped everything and neared closer to the tantalizing pouch.

He thought that the sanctum had forsaken him for good, but the documents inside proved otherwise. The holy seal confirmed its legitimacy, signed by Magistrate Mason himself. It was as he remembered them. The orders were clear and concise, even referring to him as "Paladin Brother." Reading each line of the order fervently, Baelin read the inspiring last line of the initial passage aloud, "By the power of the Magistrates, you are so ordered to fulfill your sacred oath as a soldier of God and guardian to His people."

"That sounds official." Ace Dolan jeered as he sheathed the utility knife he used to cut Spire and himself out of the netting.

Recovered from the suspended bondage, Bastian Spire crossed his arms and awaited the paladin's next move. Baelin peered at the curious soldiers, for whom he would not yet trust. It was early afternoon in the southeastern forest and he was not about to deny any guest a drink of water or a loaf of bread. Even so, he wanted to know why the New Vatican was prepared to give him a chance at redemption. It was all strangely sudden.

Arl Baelin's home was once a place of worship and forgiveness. He began living in the neglected refuge when he first discovered it, fleeing an angry mob of Islandic citizens. Upon his exile to Islandia, many saw him as a fallen soul, a defiler. It seemed as if there was no place for him, not even in his own homeland. His very presence on the island sparked a great controversy and a slew of debates. His sins were haunting.

Aggressive foliage had overtaken the basilica without mercy, making it an ideal site for a lowly paladin. Some were keen to his den of refuge and beckoned certain precautions. Baelin was a survivalist and, therefore, an expert trap maker. He lived off the land for three years, finding sanctuary in Linden on occasion. In his hometown, the paladin was openly welcomed.

"Linden." Bastian Spire began after taking a swig of fresh water from an old cup, "You have some trustworthy allies there, of that there is no doubt. They discreetly pointed us in the right direction."

Dolan followed, "It was not easy, but we found you."

Baelin strolled over and offered Dolan, like his companion, a serving of water and bread. The exhausted pair rested and indulged, admiring the inside of the basilica from an aged bench. The host stepped around his hound drinking water from a bowl and then put his back to the stoned wall, watching his guests vigilantly with arms crossed.

"How did you two merit this mission to find me?" Baelin asked, trying to hide his impatience.

Ace Dolan swallowed his bread, "We belong to a special group designed by the governor to handle sensitive operations like this one."

"Islandia appealed the New Vatican to employ you in order to solve a growing problem we have been having." Spire interjected.

"Yes, a haunting." Baelin read over the documents again, as he spoke, "This is peculiar. I have not seen this haunted mansion in my travels before. I have never even heard of it."

After wiping his mouth, Bastian Spire interlocked his fingers and brought them to his chin, saying, "Indeed. The Midvein Mansion has a certain reputation for being 'ill-disposed,' for lack of a better word. Many have said it has been haunted for decades, but only recently has the village near it claimed to have felt its supernatural spunk."

Familiarized from his papers, Baelin validated the claims, "Villagers have been missing. Tell me more about these people."

"We call them Drifters." Spire continued, "They are very simple people who keep to themselves for the most part. They travel like vagabonds about the island, as you have probably seen them. We do not really know much about them, only that it was they who initially asked us to investigate. You would want to visit them first, I would guess."

Putting the documents to rest, Baelin scrutinized his guests and said, "The soldiers that investigated — they were yours?"

Dolan answered coolly, "No, but they, and a few random curious idiots, are unaccounted for. Hence, it's your turn."

Hesitantly nodding his head, Baelin pushed himself away from the wall and sighed, "Fair enough."

"Shall we go, Ace?" Spire rose from his seat and gathered his things.

"Already?" Dolan played, "But I was waiting for the holy menu. I heard paladins make a mean liver stew."

Baelin folded his hands behind his back and faced the ancient altar to the side, clearly ignoring the heckling, "I thank you for your services. Peace be with you both."

Smiling before saluting and making his way out, Spire returned, "If you need us for anything, we shall be staying in Bayport for a while. Good luck."

Spire left, but Dolan could not help himself. Though he was willing to leave without any further quips, the marksman was star struck. Actually meeting the paladin in person, face-to-face, seized him. All of the debates and clamor that surrounded the holy knight enthralled him. Beyond the gossip, Dolan needed to know the truth from the source.

"The mace," he uttered at the basilica's assumed exit, "did you get it to light?"

Even Baelin's hound lifted his ears for the answer to this worn question. The paladin lowered his head, closed his eyes, and then turned to the Islandic soldier to say as graciously as he could, "May God be with you always."

Arl Baelin could not live in the past any longer. Yet, he had no choice, but to reminisce. It was clear to him that the path to redemption beheld his past and there was no escaping that. To rise from the ashes, Baelin, first, had to burn. Under the altar, a secret hatch led to a compartment containing a paladin's gear. At last, there was a noble purpose to equip.

The mission was, in general, self-explanatory: a haunted mansion in need of cleansing. The details of the order made the Midvein Mansion out to be a manic ward that emanated a dark presence evil enough to make villagers and soldiers vanish without a trace. Arl Baelin, as a holy knight, was sure that he had dealt with much worse. Regardless, this was his attempt to purify his name—his soul. He would endure any trial to do this, even if it meant evoking the worst of his sins.

Redeem the Knight
Atonement II

Twenty years ago...

Arl Baelin was living just inside of the Linden village district as a small boy. On this evening, an event was taking place that would change his life forever. The night was cold and wet with the smell of burning embers in the air. Holy knights from Ellium had come to bring a rogue paladin to justice, cornering him somewhere within the Linden community. By fate, the disgraced knight had taken refuge and hostages inside young Arl's home.

With his parents beaten and tied up on the floor, the rogue hid behind Arl's older sister, covering her mouth and placing an uncouth dagger to her throat. He peered outside of the window to survey the locations of the surrounding paladins looking for a peaceful way to coax him out. This felon had been on the run for weeks and chose Islandia for a place to hide. It did not work out as he had hoped.

As for Arl, he had found a hiding place of his own. Inside the kitchen closet, he gazed out at the horrifying scene and prayed that the hostile intruder did not notice him. As much as he felt to remain hidden, he wished that he had the courage to burst out and heroically save his family.   With the holy knights and villagers calling from outside and the unstable rogue pressing the knife to her delicate flesh, the situation was dangerously explosive.   Yet, something inside his spirit called on Arl to perform an act of great valor and foolishness.

While the rogue shouted and cursed at the mob outside, young Arl slowly emerged from the closet, ogling the cooking pan on the floorboards. Carefully, he squeezed his way out into the kitchen and neared closer to his desired weapon. It was a daring plan that could have led to their death. Alas, the daring plan was already doomed. Upon exiting the closet, the old hinge whined, compelling the crazed rogue to turn about and glare into Arl's innocent eyes. The intruder's mad stare froze his bones, leaving him petrified.

The look on his crazed face was obscene, like a wild animal would glower. From outside, a paladin took the chance and fired a bolt from an aiming crossbow to end the standoff. In a flash, the rogue jerked his head out of the way and let the projectile whiz through the window, emitting shards of glass on its way in. The bolt stuck deep into the wall on the far end.

The standoff was over. Moving away from the broken window, the felon gnawed his teeth and tightened his grip around her fragile neck. Arl looked into his sister's frightened eyes and then watched her cry. As a bead of sweat seeped into his left eye, the demon slit her throat and threw her stunned body to the ground. Amidst the cries of his family, Arl collapsed to his knees and froze in shock. His older sister was dead.

And still, he was not done. The monster's eyes lit up and a purple energy erupted from his open hands. The felon was more than a disgraced paladin on the run—he was a sorcerer. The killer charged up a magical incantation, fueled with anger. Arl's parents were screaming from the ground, bound and helpless to save their children.

But, the killing would not continue. A valiant paladin kicked down the door and charged the rogue in desperation. The knight rushed and tackled the killer into the kitchen table, screaming the whole way. The furniture broke and they fought on the ground, only feet away from the Baelins. The scuffle led to a bruised and battered rogue, for the knight pulled no punches and sorcery had little effect on him.

Evading arrest from his former comrade, the felon ran to the back of the house and instigated another cat and mouse chase with the paladin legion. When the hero rose to his feet, his allies had joined him in the broken home to witness the grizzly scene for themselves. A girl lay dead as a young boy began crying from his knees. The knights untied the parents and tried to console the boy. The victorious paladin moved in closer to inspect the gash in the girl's neck, but Arl mustered the will to beat him to her.

"Do not touch her!" He hollered as he caressed her cold face, "Do not touch my sister!"

Saddened by what they saw, the holy knights surrounded the boy and bowed their heads. Her father was shouting for them to heal her, as it was a possible feat for formidable paladins. But, before any one knight could attempt to revive her, Arl waved them off in sorrow and then placed his open hand over her serious wound. He cried, rocking back and forth, "Wake up, sister! Please wake up! Wake up!"

Arl's love for his sister was too great to allow her to die like this. He kept his hand on her throat tightly as he cried, forcing the blood to ooze through his fingers. For the paladin legion leader, he had seen enough. As far as he was concerned, her death was their fault. He pushed passed his allies and pulled the distraught boy from his sister's corpse. When the knights seized him, Legion Leader Mason surveyed the girl's mortal wound for himself.

To his amazement, her neck was fully healed. Blood swathed her skin, but the gash had disappeared. He could not believe it. Wiping the blood away with his cloth, the truth was clear. Young Arl Baelin somehow healed his sister. And within seconds, she coughed up lingering blood, proving that she was really alive.

With the family breaking in to embrace her, Mason stepped back and studied young Arl Baelin's reaction to his sister's revival. The outcome was unexpected. No one acknowledged the boy's magnificent deed. The paladins looked at each other and knew what they had found. It was evident that young Arl had the "blessed hand." Mason beamed, for he was actively looking for an apprentice to present to the sanctum.

Now in Linden, twenty years later…

Baelin had traveled back to Linden, his hometown, and visited the chantry to pray. He earned another chance to seek God's favor, so his spirit was anew. As a child, this was where his family had attended every Sunday. Then, he prayed for naive and simple things. Now, he prays for the opposite.

Kneeling before the altar and the crucifix, Baelin, in a faint whisper, spoke, "Lord, I beseech thee, as thy humble servant, to heed my prayer. Forgive my trespasses, as I seek to atone for my sins. May my will be strong and my heart true. May I inspire confidence and trust in my allies. Grant me the focus and valiance I shall need for this holy task. Grant me this chance, Lord. Bless my mission and my soul. I shall praise thy name to the last breath. Amen."

While he proceeded to pray in silence, a pastor approached from the side and touched his armored back. Baelin finished the Lord's Prayer and then looked over his shoulder, greeting Father Gil with a feigned smile. They both knew that a heavy throng of townsfolk had cordoned the chantry for a glance at Islandia's paladin. The chapel was quiet so that Baelin could achieve God's divine blessings in peace.

"I see the time has finally come for you." Father Gil's voice sustained a subtle echo.

Standing up and hugging his cleric and friend, Baelin said, "Thanks for the sanctuary, father."

"Nonsense," the priest replied with a smile, "you must have your wits about you now. Your presence alone gives us hope. The people need someone to look up to and that is you. "

As they walked towards the doors of the chantry, Father Gil continued, "There was no question that your prayers would be answered. It is when we challenge God, and not ourselves, that our purpose becomes skewed and we lose patience. Make no mistake—your purpose is blessed."

"And what of me?" Baelin presented a crooked grin, "After all that has happened, am I blessed?"

The priest embraced his arm and replied, "Let the people outside answer that."

After receiving a final blessing, Baelin headed for the doors and took a deep breath. This had always given him stress, staring at the windows and doors from within the chantry. It was not the outside world and it was not the throng of people awaiting him. It was the burned memory that belonged to a boy who watched a disgraced paladin slit his sister's throat right in front of him.

He could still see it all, his sister's limp body, the demon's inflamed eyes, and the people watching from outside. Yet, that was in the past. In essence, that terrifying day made him what he was today. Magistrate Mason, then a legion leader, made him what he was today. How he wished that he could be like him, a man of virtue and profound conviction.

Nonetheless, this was who he was today: a paladin in search of atonement. Gathering his valor, Baelin pushed open the doors and revealed himself to the adoring crowd outside. His admirers surrounded him in awe and reverence, distanced only by a handful of guards. Baelin nodded his head in gratitude of their support, smiling at children and shaking hands with the elderly. He had healed many of the people present at one time or another.

He was an icon here. As he made his way through the crowd, people applauded and cheered his name. Despite his dark past, Baelin was the hometown hero. They forgave his sins and trusted in his newfound purpose. However, not everyone felt this way about Islandia's paladin.

Hiding within the mob of the town square, a shady man slithered past the enthusiasts and unsheathed a jagged knife. Feeling that he was close enough, he rushed his target with a cry and plunged the blade towards Baelin's exposed neck. Just as wary bystanders noticed what was happening, Baelin turned about and snagged the assassin's armed wrist.

He then countered with his elbow and pushed the assailant back into the crowd, disarming him in the process. Guards and appalled citizens detained the man as he screamed, flailing his limbs feverishly, "Murdering pig! You fiend, may you rot in hell! You hear me? You rot in hell!"

Aghast, Baelin watched as his people dragged the howling man away until they vanished amidst the crowd. For a moment, his adoring fans were blurs in his vision. In spite of all the opposition he withstood in his life, he could never ignore how the attempts on his life from ordinary civilians affected him. Baelin pushed the confiscated knife into a guard's chest and walked on, feeling the soldier collect the weapon.

He eventually made it through the crowd, thanking them as he went, and arrived at Ronald's Rides. It was a clichéd carriage service that took one nearly anywhere about the island, as long as one was willing to pay handsomely for it. Ronald owned many carriages, large and small, and often transported travelers to Babylonia, the island's capital. For Baelin, on the other hand, the ride was always anywhere and free.

Ronald Tumbler and Arl Baelin were childhood friends— best friends. Ronald's set up was just outside of the hustle and bustle of the square, leading straight out to the east end of the town. It was where Baelin had stopped first before praying at the chantry. It was where he dropped off his personal things. In a world where it was dangerous to trust anyone, Baelin trusted him.

As Baelin neared closer to his friend's storefront, Ronald stepped into view and smirked, "The man calling you a 'murdering pig' is the same man wielding the knife. Figures."

They embraced as friends do and disappeared into the market store. As the star struck crowd began to scatter about the town again, Ronald brought his friend into the back of the shop so that they could talk. His staff knew the procedure. Business was conducted at the counters and various workers ensured that only patrons, and not paladin enthusiasts, entered the store.

While they settled in the back office, Ronald removed his gloves and sneered, "So what is this? You come down and drop off your things to pray at the chapel, or are you finally going to let me in on your new assignment?"

Shaking his head, Baelin bit back, "Word travels fast."

"Only here, Arl." Ronald sat down into a comfortable chair behind his desk and said, "So, is it true? Has the almighty Paladin's Sanctum found a purpose for you?"

Eyeing his case full of his personal equipment, Baelin retorted, "I need a ride out west."

"Where to?" He asked.

Following a brief pause, Baelin said, "You know this island better than most people. I have a good one for you."

"Try me." Ronald smiled, accepting the challenge.

Walking over to the back window, Baelin said steadily, "Ever heard of the Midvein Mansion?"

Ronald's smirk had turned to a worried stare, "You must be joking."

"There is only one joker in this room and it sure as hell isn't me." Baelin locked his hands behind his back.

"Arl," Ronald fixed his nonchalant composure, "there are certain places you just do not go to, especially if you want to run a reputable business. Midvein is psycho-town."

"Regardless of what it is, I need to be there. How close can you bring me?" The paladin asked.

Looking down at his desk as if he was suddenly overwhelmed by a heavy workload, "I—I can take you to Bayport, but—"

Baelin stepped in closer and laid his hands on the table, "Not good enough. I need to be brought in close, Ron. This may be my only chance. I can get my life back, or what's left of it."

Peering deep into his friend's eyes, Ronald reminisced on their friendship. Over the years, his business had been a safe haven for Baelin. The paladin slept there, ate there, and occasionally, unloaded and retrieved his equipment—equipment that only paladins were permitted to wield. There was a certain trust between them that could never be broken.

Giving in to his virtuous spirit, the carriage clerk replied, "Alright. Old man Chase will take you up to Drifter's Path, but that is as far as he goes. Any further and his heart will give out."

"Chase would be my first choice." Baelin grinned favorably and clasped Ronald's hand in accord, "Thank you."

Coming out from behind his desk, Ronald said, "Does this mean that you will take your holy crap out of my office for good?"

"Indeed, it does." He answered, "But I am leaving someone behind."

While watching his comrade's puzzled face, Baelin whistled for his dog. The loyal hound barked from just outside the office. Ronald shook his head in disbelief and opened the back door, letting the anxious dog scurry about. It ran to both Baelin and Ronald, jumping and bombarding them mercilessly.

Returning his friend's liking gaze while attempting to restrain the hound, Ronald barked, "Never lacking surprises."

"You know how to look after a dog, right Ron?" Baelin said, enjoying the moment.

"I should know. It was my dog." Ronald riposted.

Seizing his case and nodding his head in appreciation, the paladin said, "I will not forget this."

As he started out for the door to ask Chase for a daring ride, Ronald called him back and asked, "What did you name him?"

Referring to the dog, Baelin reflected on his choice and answered as a father, "Alec."

As children, they played in the streets of Linden, carefree and living each day to the fullest. As men, their innocence was stripped away and harmless ignorance turned into righteous rage. They found themselves living in a world where evil won the day, and heroes settled for lesser sins. Ronald had a family to care for and Baelin had his. Yet, their duties were poles apart.

The balance between father and knight took its toll on him. His ongoing battle with the Blood Reapers and healing sessions within various towns had separated him from his second responsibilities. His parents and sister moved to Ellium, where they would be part of the New Vatican. However, Baelin's wife and child lived in the outskirts of Linden, near the waterfront.

While his duties as paladin were to safeguard God's people, it was only a matter of time before he had to make a choice. It was demanding, protecting Gideon and Alec along with the common people of Islandia. In the end, the Blood Reapers made the choice for him. That was when Ronald realized that his old friend Baelin was neither a child nor a man, but a vengeful spirit.

Redeem the Knight
Resolution III

Ten years ago…

Inside the Paladin's Sanctum, a great celebration was taking place. Arl Baelin was eighteen now and his training was complete. Legion Leader Mason stood beside his apprentice, glowing with pride. They waited in the center of the holy circle for the closing stages of the splendid ritual. Arl's delighted family watched one of their own become an official paladin from outside the circle's edge.

His deeds were considered exceptional for the common population of holy knights within the Ellium Empire. The holy order was practicing for over three hundred years and Arl proved to be one of the finest pupils ever. Since the Primeval Tragedy, magical, as well as mystical, abilities had been gradually fading away, losing its prevalence in the course of generations. Yet, this boy was blessed with abilities that paladins possessed at the beginning of the order. He possessed the powers to heal mortal wounds and resist nearly all black magic.

To mark the conclusion of the rite, one of the high magistrates came forth and presented a ring. Known to the order as the "blood ring," it contained the blood of the pope and commemorated those that sacrificed their blood and their lives to God. In addition, it signified the bond that the pope and each paladin fostered from the initiation to the culmination of holy knighthood.

As it was customary, the high magistrate dressed Arl with the ring and proclaimed, "Take this ring, so that all will know that you are worthy of this hallowed sacrament. Let it be known that this man has shown compassion to the forsaken, fed the hungry, and defended the helpless. He has mastered the arts of combat, both armed and unarmed, so that no evil may trounce his resolve. Finally, as a soldier of God, he has been true to his faith. Arl Baelin, we, the High Magistrates of the Paladin's Sanctum, bless you with holy knighthood."

From the side, another magistrate handed over to the elder the Divine Mace. Appreciating that the traditional entrustment of the mace was the final phase of the rite, Arl closed his eyes and timed his breaths to avoid fainting. Mason smiled as the high magistrate finalized the ritual.

"By the power invested in the Paladin's Sanctum, we present you with the Divine Mace. We have found you worthy of the charge, but your true merit as paladin shall derive from this devout weapon." The elder raised the weapon and offered it to him, closing, "Take this blessed object as a token of your commitment to justice, charity, and purity."

Arl received the Divine Mace with great honor and humility. Finally able to feel its credence for himself, he regarded the weapon as a piece of his soul in palpable form. The mace was primarily decorated with solid silver, sporting a smooth black handle of polished hardwood that could retract and extend at the user's will. The pommel portrayed the exterior architecture of the Paladin's Sanctum and the head seemed more like a lesser spire. Emblazoned with the Paladin Coat of Arms, the crest donned six protruding points.

Upon receiving the Divine Mace, Arl watched as the head illuminated a bright bluish white, confirming its bearer's worth. The lighting of the mace was a good omen for the paladin's first wielding. It proved that the chosen knight had the love as well as the mettle to supply the sanctified mace. The audience enthusiastically applauded Arl's knighthood, acknowledging the mace's glowing crown. Indeed, this was a glorious day for the young warrior of God.

That afternoon, Arl and his close family and friends celebrated at a nearby tavern. Drinking wine and eating entrées on the house, the Baelins reveled in their son's grand accomplishments. His sister, closest to him, raised a glass and prompted others to do the same. Her following toast about his merit and benevolence touched his heart and led him to tears.

However, as the celebration continued, Mason stood in the hallway across the way and discreetly signaled that Arl come to see him there. He took him aside where it was quieter and said, "Congratulations on such an admirable feat. The heavens are rejoicing in their own taverns in the sky."

Laughing, Arl held his glass of wine in one hand and embraced his mentor's shoulder with the other, "You honor me, Sir Mason. Without you, I would not have received this regard."

Mason replied with a serious tone, "This is what I wanted to talk to you about. You remember when we first met, do you not? You remember that fateful day?"

Emulating Mason's serious tone, Arl replied, "Of course, I do. That day changed my life. It changed all of our lives."

"So you remember that disgraced paladin—the psychotic rogue that tried to—" Mason was interrupted.

"I remember, Mason." Arl tilted his head with uncertainty, "What is this all about?"

The legion leader asserted, "That man fell from grace long before we realized what you were capable of, but that does not change his significance. If he did not hold you and your family hostage that evening and attempt to kill your sister, we would never have known your potential. Your blessed powers would have gone unnoticed and people would have suffered without you. You must understand that we all serve a purpose, whether just or unjust, in shaping God's world. His fall became your rise."

Swallowing his mentor's striking words, Arl remembered that fallen paladin's eyes. It still haunted him to this day. Watching him cut into his sister's throat extenuated the feelings of fear and helplessness. But Mason was true in his reckoning, for that knight's fall was Arl's rise—trading one paladin for the other.

Then it hit him. Arl lifted his head and asked, "He ran away when you faced him, but of all the years we have known each other you never told me what happened. Mason, what did happen to that monster?"

Upon receiving the question, Mason just stared back into his eyes, taken aback. His eyes eerily widened and he began to sweat. Suddenly, Arl felt as if he was back in that house and endured a sense of insecurity he had not felt in years. Mason's eyes became so unnerving that it sent chills up Arl's spine. He never saw him like this before.

Now inside a jarring carriage, ten years later...

A loud bang and a jolt rigorously awoke Baelin from his dream. He had this dream on many occasions since his trial in the sanctum. It was a memory that his mind played back during uneasy sleeps. However, this one was different. Old man Chase had driven over an uncouth road, hitting loose rocks, and cut off Mason's recurring response.

"He suffers from a fate worse than death."

Baelin opened the shutters and peered out of the window, unable to pinpoint his location when Chase called out from ahead, "Paladin, are you awake, sir?"

"I am." He considered the dying trees along the path and the dirt road beneath the carriage, "Where are we, Chase?"

"This is where I let you off, sir." Chase slowed the carriage down to a halt and said, "This is Drifter's Path."

"So it is." Prepared to walk the rest of the way, Baelin shook off his tired spell and stepped out of the car with case in hand.

Passing the front of the carriage, he flipped a coin up to the driver and nodded. Chase received the tip well and told him to head straight down the path, for the village was just up the way. People who knew about the town named it Midvein after the historical haunted mansion just two miles away. Not many stopped by to trade, so the village was inbred with drifter culture.

Baelin started up the path, becoming familiar with the surrounding area. There were no tracks in the dirt and only a few birds graced his presence. Further he walked, until he noticed a pair of wooden spiked barriers impeding his way. He found this strange at first, but it became clear to him that the drifters did not want unwelcomed deliveries. Another spiked barrier became visible just up ahead.

In minutes, the village suddenly came into view. Conjoined by old trees, the entranceway appeared with a hooded man waiting. He wore a dark cloak and his face was barely noticeable, though he did provide a welcoming smile. The man unclasped his hands and gestured for the approaching paladin to enter the village without qualm.

"Welcome, paladin." The man said amiably, "We have been expecting your esteemed arrival."

Coming in closer to see his face, Baelin could not help but feel as if he looked familiar. There was something striking about him. He asked the man, "Have I seen you before?"

Prolonging his smile, the man replied, "My God, you remember my face? After all these years, it is a wonder."

"So we have met?" Baelin waited until the man led him into the hamlet, "From where did I see you?"

Finally leading the paladin into the town, the man said cheerily, "You healed me a while back. I had developed a terrible fever and you stripped it from me. That changed my life. My name is Cletus, by the way. Cletus Crow."

"I am Arl — " The man interjected.

"Arl Baelin, yes, we know of you." Cletus escorted him into the town, "We are grateful that you have come. Chief Hared will want to speak with you first. You can follow me."

Ambling deeper into the village, Baelin passed the watch guard station and the stable. Following the widening trail, he strolled into the middle of town, passing the blacksmith, shoemaker, clothing shack, and inn on the near left. On his far right, the church, schoolhouse, and warehouse showed signs of community structure. Other vital establishments laid about the settlement, proving the liveliness of Midvein.

The villagers were busy in their afternoon tasks, most of them wearing hoods like Cletus. The day was cool, yet hardly requiring such shrouding. They watched him like squirrels as guards followed warily from behind. It was awkwardly placid for a diligent village archetype.

Straight ahead, the Chief's Manor awaited him. Observing more of the township, Baelin looked over the path leading to the north of the village. He could see the hospital in the distance and another gate out of the region. The drifters offered the paladin scrutinizing stares and nothing more. It was as if they resented his presence, despite them asking for help.

"Many of you wear hoods or cowls." Baelin said, breaking the silence between them.

Cletus seemed prepared for the paladin's curiosity, "Well, we are drifters. Concealing our features helps us remain inconspicuous to the commoners on the outside. We are not very eager to make friends — or enemies."

"Fair enough." He replied as they walked on.

At the entrance to the Chief's Manor, two guards wielding spears glared at Baelin as he stepped inside. Within the manor, two stairways led up to the second floor, but a large pair of doors beckoned him to enter straight away. Cletus opened the double doors and gestured that his paladin guest follow. A dimly lit hall encompassed the entirety of the first floor, eventually leading him to a raised platform where the chief lingered patiently.

The closer Baelin came to the chief, the more he realized that this man was either brave in his faith or recklessly stupid. The chief was tall and sported a long scruffy beard of brown and grey. As for clothes, there was nothing impressive. He wore a green blouse and black slacks, a small improvement over his people's common attire. His stance was arrogant, even for a leader.

"Welcome, paladin, to Chimera. This is where we drifters call home. We rarely invite guests to our safe haven." He said.

Cletus bowed and presented Baelin to his superior, as the holy knight spoke, "Only when you are in dire need, I suppose. This must be strange for you—a paladin within your palisades."

Holding back ironic laughter, the chief replied, "Well, our circumstances are indeed strange enough to require your aid."

While beginning to indulge the village leader, a guard approached him and tried to take his case. Baelin instinctively rushed the case to his opposite hand and raised his pointed finger, silently warning the stewards. Another guard from behind signaled to his ally concerning a small pouch tied tightly to Baelin's belt buckle. He wanted to see what was inside.

Baelin stared at them both as the chief looked on. Losing patience with the knight, one of them pressed, "What is inside that pouch?"

"That is for me to know and for you not to know." He retorted.

"And the case?" The other insisted.

"Is mine." Baelin answered back.

An uneasy standstill persisted until Cletus slithered in to break the tension, "Surely, we can trust a paladin, sir. He is of a higher order."

Bothered by the proceedings, the chief countered sternly, "Well that would be true if he were a true paladin, Mr. Crow. I know his reputation well."

Arl Baelin scowled at the chief as he continued, "He is a fallen paladin. This is his first solicited mission in three whole years. This is his chance to show his merit. Believe me, paladin, we know who you are and what you did. If we are to trust you, we must know more about you."

Incensed, Baelin put down the case and opened it just enough to take out confidential documents given to him by the New Vatican. He raised it up and said, "This is all you need to know. You asked for hallowed services and I, a true paladin, heeded the call. The New Vatican and the Paladin's Sanctum have trusted in me to fulfill this holy quest. If you choose to refuse my aid, then I suggest you start praying. I am willing to help you now. Are you willing to accept my help?"

A heated chief re-joined, "That depends on what you call 'help.' I recall a witch that once hunted people suspected of Blood Reaper affiliation. I recall you intervening with her bold actions and killing her in the process. Is that the aid a true paladin is willing to bestow upon us?"

"Your recollection needs work." Baelin answered, "The Witch of Swamp Hill was killing anyone suspected of being a Blood Reaper, not Blood Reapers. There is a difference. Her methods were sadistic and unreliable. And for your personal records, I did not kill her."

"Then what happened to her, paladin? She just vanished into oblivion?" The chief lifted up his arms in disgust.

"That does not concern you." Baelin raised his voice, "What should concern you is a house that is responsible for various disappearances of your villagers, Islandic citizens, and soldiers. That is why I am here, so can we debate about false rumors some other time? I would like to do some holy work."

Another pause. The chief and paladin glowered at each other long enough to make the village spectators wary. Their stalemate in philosophy produced a silent spectacle, compelling the guards to prepare for anything. They watched as the chief stepped down from the platform with his ensuing glare and loomed towards Baelin.

Although he had a fiery temper, Chief Hared broke out in strange laughter as he advanced, "Well, what can I do? We are desperate for holy intervention and a priest will not do in this case. Since the New Vatican has sent you, I must be thankful. We all serve a particular purpose, no? You have yours and I have mine."

When they were finally face-to-face, Baelin returned coolly, "Alright. Perhaps you would be kind enough to guide me to the cursed mansion?"

"Of course," he said, "it is just up north a ways. The mansion, however, is not cursed — it is haunted. It is haunted by a horrible ancient demon, so I would recommend that you sleep here tonight and ride out in the morning."

"I appreciate your hospitality, but I will be sleeping inside the mansion." Baelin said while tending to his case.

Amongst the gasps and baffled faces, Cletus uttered, "What? Are you mad?"

Baelin answered, "I have heard enough of this place. I want to see it for myself from the inside out."

When it was clear that the paladin was ready to leave, the chief laughed again and walked him towards the doors, "So be it! You are either brave or psychotic. I would rather wager that you are both. I like that. At the very least, will you eat something?"

"If you can spare it, I'll take something for later." Baelin said as he left the manor, "I expect to cleanse the Midvein Mansion in a day's time."

With Cletus Crow at the paladin's side, the chief declared, "For a paladin, we will provide a hefty satchel of rations. Mr. Crow will escort you up to the lovely portal of hell, and if you survive the night, we will discuss your discoveries over a hot breakfast tomorrow morning."

Baelin did not approve of the chief's awkward dealings with him. He stared at him diligently before walking off with Cletus. Leery villagers ogled the paladin as he headed towards the market strip for foodstuff and equipment. Chimera's chief, like his people, watched Baelin very carefully. Welcoming outsiders was always a risk. However, for some, welcoming Arl Baelin, the infamous paladin, was reckless.

Later in the day...

Strolling up the north path towards the Midvein Mansion was dangerous in the late afternoon. Baelin, wielding resolution, walked with Cletus and meditated on his mission. The village herald had made this trip many times, but only up to the sighting of the mansion. He would not escort the paladin all the way, for doom awaited any who dared to test its malevolence.

Feeling to speak, Baelin said as he marched, "I did not care very much for your leader's disdain."

Cletus, surprised by the paladin's comment, rejoined, "You must forgive him for that. He means to defend us from any outside threats, even from a holy man such as yourself."

"That's fine," Baelin countered, "but it was more than that. He doubted my honor. He mentioned the Witch of Swamp Hill even, as if to intentionally anger me with gossip."

"It was his way of testing you." Cletus uttered without emotion, "This debacle has made us all quite weary, I'm afraid."

"He wanted to kill and kiss me in the same discussion." Baelin continued, "I will count on your council from now on, Cletus. Your chief did not earn my trust."

Cletus Crow did not say anything. Instead, he watched the rising path's horizon like a deer scouting for predators. The trees along the road were dead and the grass was like hay. Even Baelin could sense that the notorious mansion was near. He felt an oppressive sensation in his chest and a rise at the back of his neck. Suddenly, they both were able to see the archaic roof and pair of chimneys. That was enough for one of the travelers.

Slowing down and becoming fidgety, Cletus uttered, "That's the place right there. That is Midvein Mansion. Good luck, paladin, this is as far as I go."

The village herald bowed speedily before running off. Baelin watched him sprint back towards the village, leaving before the house could see him. For a man who lived in Islandia for most of his life, Baelin could not comprehend why he never heard of this infamous site before. Clearly, those who knew about the mansion feared its every fiber. He would have to familiarize himself with the notorious place to be certain of its authenticity.

Yet, upon seeing the house, a grave impression seized him. The Midvein Mansion was ancient indeed. It seemed to live upon the hill like a sleeping demon waiting for a doomed passerby. Baelin stopped in his tracks and considered the large edifice. The exterior was beaten and worn by the elements of the ages. An old rusting gate, overrun by the dead creeping plants of yesteryear, dared him to pass through.

The visage of the mansion was left untouched for decades. Some first floor windows were warped and fogged out, barely concealing what lurked inside the house. The most disturbing attributes of the place, however, were the front doors. As old as they appeared, a curious haze emitted from underneath. With the paladin looking on, the haze formed into an apparition of a man.

Baelin squinted to confirm that his eyes were not playing tricks. The ghostly figure simply stood there at the entrance to the mansion and slowly pointed in the opposite direction, passing over the village of Chimera. His ethereal eyes peered into Baelin's soul in the meantime. It was chilling.

Then, the ghost shook his head, warning the holy knight to stay away. Before Baelin could fully believe what he saw, the apparition was sucked back into the house with tremendous force. Like a vacuum, the ghost vanished behind the doors, leaving Baelin to stand alone at the mansion's entrance and marvel at the realization of his new quest. At last, the advice he received about Midvein Mansion seemed alarmingly plausible.

Redeem the Knight
Fear IV

Five years ago…

Deep within the forest of western Islandia, a small encampment of gypsies took refuge by the tributary. The watercourse then proceeded to empty into a large lake, serving as their fishing and bathing place. Arl Baelin, now an esteemed paladin, braved the river with a small rowboat to reach the camp. He was not on a quest, nor was he performing a holy task. Arl came to Swamp Hill to visit his new love, Gideon.

Swamp Hill was a placid marsh near the encampment where gypsies went to practice the magical arts. Of all the occultists who lived there, only Gideon was considered exceptional. She dabbled in the dark arts since she was just a child. Now, as a young woman, she was a magician—a formidable witch. Regardless of these heretical talents, Arl loved her.

He found her one year earlier, tied to a stake and surrounded by zealots outside of a small Seafare village. Atop of horses then, Arl and his comrade noticed the suspicious invocation. When they reached her, the fire had already been set. Arl leapt from his steed and broke through the throng to save her.

His ally broke up the mad "witch hunt," as it was, and demanded that everyone disperse. The paladins warned them that such actions were profane and not tolerated by God. The accused witch was faintish. Arl laid her on a bed within the village for means of resuscitation as his ally kept watch. From the moment Gideon could focus in on her rescuer, their connection had already begun to flourish.

To this day, they have met within the gypsy camp in secret to protect their love from the eyes of the enemy and of his allies.

It was blasphemous for a paladin, or any man of the blessed faith, to court a witch. And yet, Arl defied these laws. They were in love and he knew that love could not be contained by the tenets of man.

Passing by welcoming crowds within the encampment, Arl docked at Swamp Hill. There Gideon waited for her lover's embrace once again. Her long black hair cascaded down her pale shoulders. She wore a grey blouse with a purple sash tied around her waist. As a witch, she possessed various power bracelets and spell rings. As a woman, Gideon reached out for the paladin who loved her.

They kissed fervently and proceeded to seek privacy in her hut. After moments of passion, they nestled in her bed and held each other close. The forbidden pair remained silent for a short while, reveling in each other's presence. In due course, Gideon asked about his adventures. He told her stories and she pressed herself deeper into his arms.

Soon after their romantic exchange, Gideon caressed his hand that hugged her chest and said hesitantly, "Arl, I must tell you something, but I do not know how you will take it."

He squeezed her exposed arm and endearingly replied, "You know you can always speak your mind with me."

She turned about to face him on her side and mustered the courage to say, "I performed an incantation last week. My blood and my bones told me the truth about my aches—about my hunger."

"Are you sick? I can heal you. I told you that." He said before she could finish.

"No, that is not it." She nipped, "Arl, I am pregnant."

She breathed deeply after admitting her findings and continued, "We have eight months more and I will give birth to a boy. You will be a father."

Arl was instantly taken by her revelation, unable to speak right away. He read the joy and fear in her eyes as he thought of a worthy response. The stark realization hit him. A holy knight created life with a witch. Mason, newly instated as a magistrate, warned him of this. If he knew what Arl had done, he would have been mortified.

Nevertheless, he knew the consequences of loving Gideon. He made his choice and was willing to pay any price. Now, he was a father. He had a deeper purpose to live. At last, his duties as a paladin were no longer enough. He had to shield his new family from all harm at all costs.

She touched his face, asking, "Will you at least say something?"

Arl could only say, "I have never been so scared in all of my life. I am overjoyed and petrified all at once. How do you know that it is a boy?"

"I just know." Gideon answered, refraining from sharing her sorcerous methods of affirmation.

Then Arl shed a tear and forced a smile, "I will never let anything happen to you. That is my eternal pledge to the both of you."

"I can take care of myself." She retorted, "It is this child that we must protect. How will you hide him from the sanctum? If they find out, they will take him away from us!"

"No, that will not happen, Gideon. Don't even say that." He said.

"But you know it's true. We have enemies and they will try to find us. I do not care who it is, whether it is a Blood Reaper, a governor, or a priest. If they hurt my child, I will kill them." She avowed.

"Stop it!" Arl seized her from the back of the head, "Gideon, stop saying these things. I will not allow anything or anyone to afflict my family. Do you understand me?"

Swallowing nervously, she said in a calmer tone, "I trust you, but I know the world better than you do. You have the backing of the New Vatican. You have clear adversaries. As for me, I have no clear adversary. I fear the paladins just as much as the Blood Reapers.

"I need you to recognize that you have fallen in love with someone who possesses dark magic. How can I leave this place now after all that has happened in the past? This is my home now. Will we hide our child like the rest of us here? Does he deserve to be imprisoned in this cursed swamp? I fear that our love will not be strong enough to protect him from the entire world."

Taking a deep breath, Arl held her tight and whispered, "God will keep us safe."

Gideon shook her head in apprehension, before gently kissing his hand, "Trade fear for faith.' Paladin, is that your answer?"

"Trade fear for faith." Arl proceeded to caress her hair as he replied quietly, "That is my life."

Now at Midvein Mansion, five years later...

The main doors to the mansion opened sternly, bellowing old dust and wood particles about the atrium. Baelin stood in the midst of the darkened house as a silhouette from the outside looking in. He let his eyes adjust to the dark as he opened up his clandestine chest. From inside, he pulled out the Divine Mace and held it before him.

With confidence, he closed his eyes and swallowed his fears, trusting in the powers of God. He emptied what remaining purity he had left into the mace and used it as a torch in the darkness, lighting up the weapon's head. The light was bright, yet not irritating. It illuminated the first floor of the house and revealed the ancient architecture. Instantly, he was certain that spirits watched him.

Cobwebs consumed the chandelier, while lamps on the walls were snuffed out. Dust visibly drifted passed Baelin and his glowing mace as he crept deeper into the house. As expected, he could hear the clambering of unseen spirits on the stairs and prattling voices all about him. He explored the mansion cautiously, experiencing brief encounters of ghosts on his way. They watched him for now.

Baelin had visited many haunted places before such as caves, cemeteries, and derelict roads. This place, however, was eerily unique. There was a great hatred and sadness emitting from lonely halls and rooms. Baelin was fighting the cowering itch. His bravery was dour, but the aura of Midvein Mansion took its toll on his soul. The sensation was ever-present.

The hallway of old red carpet led to a sitting room and cocktail lounge fit for a prince. He followed the bannister down to the lower level of the hall, meeting the end of the red carpet at the end of the stairway. Peculiar paintings and life-size statues were all about the place, some idolizing prominent people and events of the old world — the world before the Primeval Tragedy hit.

Another grand chandelier resided above, this one bigger than the first. As he walked through the hall, Baelin was in awe of its unnerving dereliction. Almost like it was alive, seeking to accommodate guests who shall never come. He could imagine the bustling scene here so many years ago. From this chamber, branches of other corridors tempted the paladin to explore the interior of the mansion further.

Nonetheless, Baelin wished to climb to the third and highest floor of the house, seeking the master bedroom. From there, he would perform the cleansing sacrament. He let his mace guide him throughout the mansion, serving as the light in the dark that shrouded creeping spirits. Paintings on the walls of corridors seemed to stare at him. Occasional statuettes provided the same tingling service.

Reaching the third level, Baelin ambled down the hallway and passed by three rooms before reaching the largest. The master bedroom was elaborate with various dressers and drawers, a workstation, a large oval window looking out at the front of the mansion, and a king sized bed. The bathroom had a tub, sink, and toilet — all which were useless after the apocalypse.

The paladin placed his trunk at the foot of the bedstead and laid the Divine Mace on its side on top of the desk. He then peered out at the world outside from the master window, watching all the crows perch on the fence below. Baelin would perform the rite tonight and banish the restless spirits from within. Before that, however, a late afternoon meal was in order.

He opened the sack of food and ate at the workstation, reading over the cleansing ritual from his case. While the feeling of prying ghosts lingered, Baelin had not been bothered as of yet. The house was still investigating him just as he was investigating it. The evening was cool and obscure. The crows were gone and the mansion was oddly quiet. It was time to start the rite.

Cleanse the house of evil spirits and return to Chimera. That was all he had to do to step back into the light of the sanctum. It would take more than that to step back into the light of the heavens. Baelin opened his case, took out a dangerously elaborate knife, and placed it on the desk beside the Divine Mace. He then removed an old battered bible. The holy book was considered the most powerful book of the age, for it was in short supply in a forsaken time. Finally, Baelin retrieved the Compendium, a guidebook, or manual, for paladins only.

It was the Holy Bible and Compendium he needed for the cleansing. He kneeled on the floor and prayed to God to bless him with valiance, will, and focus. It had been a long time since he performed this rite, so Baelin was rightfully uneasy. Already sweating, he placed the two books at his sides and positioned the candles around him. He raised his arms and initiated the ritual.

With his eyes closed, Baelin could sense that the old mansion had a sinking foundation, causing a slight slant. As he proceeded with the rite, a bloodcurdling cry sounded from downstairs. Baelin opened his eyes wide, for it disrupted his concentration. The scream was vibrant. "Help me! No!" There was a subtle thump after the man's desperate plea.

The cry would have sent chills up anyone else's spine, but paladins were keen to manifestations such as this. Regardless, Baelin had the urge to postpone the ritual and scrutinize the alarming cry. It sounded so real that it could have belonged to a living person. He took the mace with him and left the master bedroom.

From the guest rooms to the music room and the dining hall to the vintage library, Baelin checked everywhere for the source of the scream. At night, the mansion held a much more sinister energy. As brave as he was, he still caught himself frequently looking over his shoulder. He found nothing thus far. Clearly, this was a spirit's rendition of a moment in time.

Standing alone in the atrium where he previously entered the mansion, Baelin was hearing something else. Heavy, slow footsteps resounded from the upstairs, making the floorboards creek. Someone, or something, was playing a mean trick. He sprinted back up to the third floor and noticed a small figure rounding the corner before him. Judging from the light of the mace and the sharpness of his eye, it looked like a small child.

"Wait!" Baelin called in a whisper and pursued the girl. Back on the third floor hallway, there were the sounds of someone running towards him. He stood his ground and permitted the oncoming sounds to race passed him, holding the mace tightly. Haunted, Baelin cautiously made his way to the master bedroom only to discover a chilling message.

On the door, written in blood, read, "You will burn."

It looked like it was traced with two fingers practically dripping with blood. Though he looked, there were no clues as to how this was done. He could not determine if the message was a direct threat, but was sure that the ghosts of the mansion would fill him in during the dead of night.

Late at night…

Baelin had finished the cleansing rite without any further distractions, implementing texts from the Holy Bible and the Compendium, blessing the house with holy water, and using his powers to flush out any evil influence. After wiping his brow with a cloth, he waited for any haunting signs from outside of the bedroom. There was nothing, though the sensations did not seem to lift. The sinister feeling remained.

There was a clap of thunder outside, lighting up the dimly lit room for a brief second. The candles warmly lit the place, adding a small level of peace to a disturbing ambiance. Exhausted from the sacrament, Baelin performed the sign of the cross and thanked God for the stamina. He removed the bedroll from his case, finally emptying its contents completely. Baelin would try to find respite now, though not within the dusty sheets of an antique mattress. Silently, he whispered another prayer, hoping that his holy actions were taking shape within the haunted mansion.

In the master bed, his thoughts were racing. Gideon and Alec appeared in his mind as always before falling asleep. While seeking forgiveness from God, he also prayed that they would as well. It hurt him so, nearly every night, whether under the open sky or inside a derelict mansion. The memories of his lost life cursed him. Thinking of how he let Mason and his family down back in Ellium was commonplace. Ultimately, Baelin would have to forgive himself first—and he could not do that.

However, in the middle of the night, a bare clue to the house's resistance materialized. He woke up to a baleful feeling in his lower chest. From behind the bedroom door and below, two feet settled in. Adjusting his tired eyes, Baelin could see them now, facing his door from the hallway. Then came the heavy knocking, like a battering ram.

Every two seconds, the door shook in its hinges from the massive force of the spirit's knocking—if it was indeed a spirit. Baelin rested his head down onto the pillow and sighed, realizing now that the cleansing spell did not work. He reached over to the left side to recover his mace from the bed table, when he felt another sensation behind him. Looking to his right, he was certain that there was someone standing over the bed.

Amidst the prolonged banging, Baelin shone the light of the Divine Mace to see what it was. In the glow, a girl stared at him with beaming eyes. He was not alone any further and it startled him. Unable to speak now, he just clenched the mace tightly and returned her glare until she spoke, "I'll be right back."

She ran off towards the rattling door and walked right through it, compelling the nerve-racking knocking to cease. This was his punishment for not thinking deeper—for forgetting the truths about cleansing rites. There was a source of evil inside the mansion somewhere immunizing itself against exorcisms. Like doctors staving off an infection, any cures are futile unless they strike at the source. The questions then surfaced: What was the source and where was it?

From in the hallway, the girl's incessant sobbing replaced the knocking. She must have been just outside of the door. Finding it unbearable, Baelin squirmed out of bed and walked right out into the hallway. Even with the mace's magnificent glow, he saw nothing. The sobbing stopped, and he was unhinged. He waltzed down the corridor a few paces before exhaling with exuberance. This strategy of chasing down spirits was attempted before.

Feeling to return to the master bedroom, Baelin turned back and stopped dead in his tracks, for the girl was right in front of him. His heart skipped a beat. As he backed away slowly, the girl looked at him as if to plea for help and whined, "I'm sick."

Just then, she rolled back her eyes and opened up her mouth wide, regurgitating an army of black spiders that crawled all about her face and neck. The arachnids scrambled down her body and onto the floor heading towards Baelin directly. Aghast, the paladin backed away and then ran to the nearest door of the hallway, forcing himself into it. He shut it and gave room, watching the relentless spiders quickly creep in from under the chamber door.

He hastily swiped at the ethereal critters with his mace primarily out of desperation. The Divine Mace, of course, was intended to handle flustering adversities such as these. The hallowed light burned them like figs in a bonfire. Repeatedly, he swung at the spiders, delivering them all to ash on the floor. He did this until there were no more of them left. Baelin breathed in deep and tried to shake away the jitters.

The house was not finished yet. From behind him, another spirit materialized—a different one. Baelin turned about to witness a knife-wielding ghost face the mattress, stricken with madness. He backed away from the specter and scrutinized the room for which he was in. This was the little girl's bedroom and that was her bed. Quiet now, he watched as the translucent man played with the knife in his trembling hand, mumbling incoherent things.

"She has to die, you understand? It must die with her!" The spirit cried out in a fury, "It must die!"

He turned to face Baelin there and lunged for him, possessed with lunacy. Before the paladin could know how to react, the ghost plunged the knife into his chest. Baelin gasped as the blade pierced his body. It felt real. He rushed backwards and placed his hand over the suspected wound. When the man tried for a second strike, he swung the Divine Mace for his head.

Upon contact, the ghost's head vanished to a lingering haze. Baelin then shouted and delivered a final blow to the torso, turning the spirit's transient figure into a floating orb of spectral matter. He then checked his own torso only to find that the strike from the spirit's blade caused an angry burn in his bare chest. It was sensitive to the touch. The inhabitants of Midvein Mansion were not common specters by the era's standards. These ghosts were severely troubled and very much capable of killing him.

He had seen enough. Baelin kicked open the door and marched into the hallway, seeing nothing and not becoming fooled by it. Wielding the mace without his armor, he returned to the master bedroom and headed towards the oval window. The skies were still stormy. The lightning — still striking.

From all about the house now, several spirits were calling in unison: "Get out! Leave her and get out! Run away! Get out!"

Listening to the demoralizing cries of the damned spirits, Baelin ogled the door that he left ajar and waited for something to come for him. He watched it devotedly, for he was certain that he would have another visitor. When phantom fingers wrapped themselves around the frame of the door to reveal a sneaking head from the side, Baelin clenched his teeth. From the unrelenting haunts to the demoralizing demands for him to leave, all that he could think about now was leaving.

The bible sat on the bed table. While the Divine Mace was a match for the ghosts on the physical plane, the holy book was the greater article. He took the bible in his other hand and dared the apparition to challenge him. Among the fleeting strikes of the storm, the paladin and the prying ghost gawked at one another.

He recited the Lord's Prayer, a Hail Mary, and the Compendium's protective spell. They proceeded to watch each other further. It was only until Baelin approached it and growled, "Be gone, spirit," that it had drifted back into the recesses of the otherworld. Many warned him that this place was not to be taken lightly. He saw it for himself. Now, he had to find the source of the hauntings and put an end to it. Baelin was not the type to be broken easily, but neither was Midvein Mansion.

Redeem the Knight
Reckoning V

Three years ago…

Arl and Gideon married in the gypsy camp one fine Sunday under the clear blue sky, surrounded by those that reveled in their love for each other. There was a peaceful ceremony and a joyful reception. As a paladin, he had hoped that his immediate family and members of the sanctum could have come to the precious wedding, but their marriage had to be kept a secret. Nonetheless, it was still one of the happiest days of their lives.

Seven months later, their infant was born and Arl named him Alec after his grandmother, Alexandria.   They lived as wedded parents within the forest, spending days and nights together as a loving family. Residents of the swamp put their efforts together to help Gideon care for the baby when Arl was gone. He found it awfully challenging to be apart from them while at the Paladin's Sanctum or on missions. He wondered sometimes, as Gideon did, if their secret life would one day come crumbling down.

Tonight, that fear had finally come to fruition. They tied him up like a pig, his wrists ensnared from the back and his ankles bound. A thick rag gagged him, as he was only able to bite down on the fibers. Around his eyes, they tied a blindfold. The poison was a commonly used toxin among Blood Reapers. Arl could taste it on his tongue. Paladins were impervious to most toxins, for the sanctum trained holy knights to eradicate such contaminants from the body. Yet, this brew was modified to last within a paladin's system for longer.

All that he could remember was the initial onslaught from a psychotic band of Blood Reapers. They had tracked him to the camp somehow, wishing to ruin his life forever. Arl was their nemesis in Islandia and they had tried many times to kill him. In his fervor to return home to his wife and son, Arl led his worst enemies to where they hoped he would. Unmistakably, he was in their clutches and approaching death. But what of his family?

He could hear them around what must have been a campfire. They were laughing and cursing. He heard his own name a few times. Grinding his head about the ground, Arl was able to move the blindfold just above his right eye. Fighting the urge to fall back into a deadly sleep, the doomed paladin saw the vile assassins. He was right. They were Blood Reapers.

Three sat on the ground, while a heavier one sat up in a chair around the campfire. The wide mouth was gloating over the paladin's defeat while the other three listened in, too eager to be called warriors. The seated slob went on about how he was part of the ambush. He helped raid the camp and destroy the paladin's secret world. Arl could do nothing but listen in to the cruel and sadistic account.

A massive member of the reapers, a robust savage, attacked him first. That was the last he could remember. The slob was very graphic in describing his role in Gideon's rape. How he enjoyed her cries and faltered attempts to fight back. They then slit her throat and left her for dead in the swamp. Her child was given no latitude. The monster offered a triumphant smile when explaining the murder of Arl's son, swung about like a doll until they bashed his head onto a rock.

Amongst the laughter and cheers around the campfire, Arl's blood boiled. He gnawed on the gagging rag like an enraged beast lusting for blood. Through his one eye, he watched them guffaw and drink to his suffering. He charred every face into his mind. They destroyed his life—his spirit. The Blood Reapers were occultists and cannibals, but not cold blood murderers.

These thugs were of a different breed. Someone ordered them to perform this vile deed. Arl was intent on finding this someone. He was ravening to find him. There was nothing left, but retribution. Forgiveness could wait. He was going to catch the man responsible for this and make him pay, no matter what the cost. First, he had to attain some useful information. That fat murdering rapist liked to talk. Arl was going to make him talk a whole lot more — like his life depended on it.

He heard everything down to the last grisly detail. Come morning, the three reapers were to collect the paladin and deliver him, dead or alive, to a contact. That contact would then transfer him to the alleged leader of the Blood Reapers. Arl would make sure that the racketeer received a very different package. The thugs were asleep now. It was time to act.

After an hour's struggle of breaking free from his bondage, Arl knelt down and vomited. His stomach was in knots from the toxin. His skin was on fire. There the four brutes slept peacefully, but not for long. Arl pulled one of them up by his hair and covered his mouth. When he awoke in shock, the paladin broke his neck and threw him to the ground.

The next two suffered the same fate, ensuring that there would be no delivery. Arl let the fire burn. He wanted to see the man's face clearly. Therefore, he sat his drunken frame back onto the chair and bound his ankles and wrists to the wooden legs. Not until Arl slapped him across the face did he awaken, scared and traumatized.

"No!" The man gulped, "What the hell is going on?"

Facing the fire, the obese offender had become the victim. Arl sat across from him and peered into the flames, watching the man try to break free to no avail. The poison was still coursing through his veins, compelling Arl to play with his eyes in order to stay focused.

"Where are my things?" Arl asked, frozen with ire.

Shaken, the man jerked his head to the left, revealing the location of Arl's armor and trunk. After a long insufferable pause, he asked the bound man, "Who gave you the order to do this—to kill my family? I want you to tell me who your leader is right now. If you don't, I will kill you."

"Then kill me and be done with it!" He cried, "No one knows the leader of the reapers!"

Arl rose from the dirt and ambled over to him, nearing in extra close to growl, "I heard what you did. I heard everything. How you gloated, how you laughed. May God have mercy upon me for what I am willing to do if I don't get an answer."

Stammering first, the man quickly replied, "No, I didn't do any of those things! He wanted to hear what we did to you and your family, so I told them lies—exaggerations!"

Looking deep into his eyes, Arl backed up and delivered a defining punch to his face. The man yelped and fell to the floor, chair and all. Arl picked him back up and said, "I believed you the first time. Now, you don't sound so convincing."

"Go to hell! You deserved every bit of what you got! You and your whole family!" He shouted his last protest.

Taking a deep breath and holding his heart, still fighting the poison, Arl grunted, "Fine."

From behind, he leaned the chair over the fire with his foot, letting the reaper cry out in horror. Any further, and the chair would have toppled over into the blaze. He surrendered and spewed up all he knew about the plot. He mentioned a pub in Whitestone where he was given the assignment of transporting Arl's body to this precise location. That was what he knew.

"If I go to this pub and find that you lied to me, I will be very displeased. So displeased that I will hunt you down and finish what I started." The paladin said, fighting back tears,

"Better yet, I'll give you the same chance you gave my wife and infant child."

Without hesitation, he kicked the chair over and sent the screaming reaper face first into the campfire. The flames roared as he squirmed and cried to a whimper. Arl left him to die as he stammered over to the wagon that held his things. The horses that he did not notice at first started to jerk themselves from the harnesses. He released three to the wild and left one for himself.

He bolted on the reaper's horse like a racing equestrian, headed for Swamp Hill. Arl had to make sure. He had to search for Gideon's body, and for his son's. In the middle of the night, dismayed gypsies witnessed the paladin they knew so well gallop through in search of his family. They tried to warn him, but he just rode deeper into the marshland.

Occupants of the raided camp came to see the paladin fall to his knees and cry at the lake. There was no sign of his family, only accounts from the residents there. The Blood Reapers finally found a way to crush his noble spirit, by way of his heart. It was then when he realized that he had been playing the wrong game. The reapers needed a taste of their own vile medicine. This was how they would learn never to harm others the same way.

Arl took to the road again, despite the gypsies' appeals to rest. He rode all the way to Whitestone, a popular city in the Riverhead County. There was no stopping him now. As a raider himself, Arl moved through the darkness of night to find the location of the obscure pub. He knew about the bar's significance better than some Blood Reapers. It served as a safe house for them. Some also came to do business or deliver messages.

In disguise, Arl surveyed the bar for three straight days, learning who the real reapers were and what they were doing there. Patience had proved to be virtuous when he tagged one of the reapers as a raider on that ominous evening. He struck then, barreling through any opposition. Arl burst into the pub and incapacitated any challengers. They were no match for him, for he was on a quest for vengeance.

When others learned not to tangle with him, the paladin moved over to the arrogant reaper drinking his hard liquor at the bar table. Arl knocked the glass from his fingers and slammed his head onto the counter, putting one arm in a painful lock. The reaper coughed, "Whoever you are, you're dead!"

"You should have been more careful." He said, "I remember your repulsive face at my home! You talk: you walk. You don't: you die."

"If you're Baelin, don't try to scare me. Holy lackeys like you don't kill anyone." The reaper grumbled.

Wrong answer. After being thrashed about the pub, turning the place into a trench, he decided to blurt out the evasive contact's name. Arl let the thug live in anguish and humiliation as a reward. When he left, patrons of the wrecked pub were staggered and silent. They had never seen Islandia's paladin like that before. They could not have known how far he was willing to go to make the Blood Reapers pay.

Arl tracked the contact for hours until he visited a brothel in Bayshore. The descriptions of this reaper were dead on. It was surprisingly easy to find him. He must have been anxious all day upon his discovery that the emissaries were dead and the paladin was gone. While he would have liked to let off some steam, Arl wished to make his day one he would not soon forget.

When the reaper entered the private room for his fix, his package hid behind the door. Arl snared him from behind and put him into an excruciating headlock. As much as he fought, there was no way of breaking out of it. A frightened woman cowered in the corner by the bed. Arl interrogated the reaper viciously until there was no way for him to answer at all.

Wrathful, the paladin inadvertently snuffed him out. Any clues to their leader's location were lost.

The harlot hiding in the corner was frantically praying to God, lowering her head between her knees and shaking. His act of murder terrified her. For all his life, Arl had lived to inspire hope and justice—not this. There was no turning back now. He had already done so much. Catching his breath, he came closer, unsure of how to console the woman. Kneeling there, he hushed her and apologized for what she saw.

He tried to console her as paladins do, but there was no use in this. There were no paladins in that place. The virtues of justice, charity, and purity were replaced by hatred, revenge, and imprudence. Arl started to cry again, trounced by his spiraling world. The woman took a chance and scurried for the door. Yet, when freedom was promising, she turned back and considered the wretched scene. Arl Baelin recoiled beside the bed and wept into his hands.

She heard his questions and knew the slain reaper by name. They all knew the reaper here, for this was not only a brothel, it was a Blood Reaper haven. Though scared out of her mind, the woman closed her eyes and mustered the courage to utter wanly, "Upstairs."

Arl wiped away his tears and tried to listen to what the woman said, as he thought she already ran away. She pointed to the celling and said louder, "He is sleeping upstairs."

The sadness was gone. He finally realized where he was and why she was eager to help him. The leader was here and vulnerable. If she was lying, then Arl would be trapped within a reaper sanctuary. If she was telling the truth, then vengeance was his. The unforgiving paladin rose to his feet and clenched his fists. This was where the path of reckoning ended.

Vane Brandon, an infamous leader of the Blood Reapers, slept peacefully in his bed. The room was dark and only a weak beam of light crept through the crevasse of the door. Something compelled him to awaken. He caressed his bald head and groaned, "Who's there? Show yourself!"

From the obscurity of the dark, a voice obliged, "Yes, I will show myself to you. You deserve to see your mistake."

Arl lifted the Divine Mace and gave light to the room, revealing his face. Brandon, startled by the glowing mace, concealed his eyes. He realized who made it to his quarters. The contact enlightened him of the mission failure and warned that this day might come. As a prominent figure of the reapers, he should have been sooner to act.

"By coming here, you think that you will prove something? What a—" Brandon's pride was costly. Arl cut off his smug rant with a club to the skull. His head opened up before it hit the floor, splattering blood all over the wall and furniture. And there the paladin stood, alone with a corpse and a bloody consequence. The illusive man he hunted so keenly was dead. Slowly, the brilliant light of the Divine Mace began to fade until it died out completely, leaving Arl in the dark room alone and without grace.

In Chimera, three years later …

Early morning, the chief supervised villagers set four tombstones in the cemetery. From behind them, Cletus Crow came forth with Arl Baelin to his right. Baelin, adorned in his battered armor, left his trunk inside the mansion. His stature was dreary, for his waking nightmare did not merit him much rest. A guard alerted the chief to their coming.

Without turning around to greet him, Chief Hared said haughtily, "Ah, welcome back, paladin. How marvelous that you survived the night at Midvein Mansion. As promised, I shall have my subordinates prepare a hot breakfast for you so that we may discuss what you have discovered from the 'inside-out,' as you put it."

Baelin swallowed what he really wanted to say and asked instead, "What, in God's name, happened in that house?"

"I was hoping you could tell me, paladin." The chief turned to face him.

"Don't play with me." Baelin countered, "You could have warned me about, say, ghosts that could potentially stab me or girls that throw up spiders."

"I see you have met Sarah." The chief replied insouciantly.

Affronted, Baelin clasped his hands behind him and said, "Evidently, you know more about this place than you led on. If you want me to cleanse that house, you need to pull your weight. Something terrible happened in that mansion—something that you know."

"You look dog-tired." The chief remarked as he inspected the paladin's aura.

Without emotion, Baelin answer back, "I didn't sleep much last night."

As the villagers were working on the final stages of the gravestones, Chief Hared took a moment and said, "You see these? They are the empty graves of our missing people. We may be simple rustics to you, but we want the same thing everyone else wants out there. Remember to show us a little respect, paladin. It is time that you learned what we know, now that you have found use for us."

The chief started to walk back towards his manor when Cletus signaled for Baelin to follow. He took a last look at the graves before walking off, remembering why he was here. Every villager offered him a look to remember whilst catching up to the chief's snail pace. Cletus, under the shroud, followed closely behind them.

Once Baelin neared his side, the chief resumed, "That house is older than you may think. It lasted the apocalypse nearly six hundred years ago. You can think of it as a living monument—a reminder of the sins of our past. Where is your fancy case?"

"It is safe." He answered, "I performed a cleansing ritual from the master bedroom and it had no effect. There must be a source of its evil power stemming from somewhere. I could not find any such place."

"After what I show you, you may not want to search for this place." The chief retorted.

After they reached the manor, Baelin and the chief stepped into the dining room. Cletus remained outside and gently closed the door, watching Baelin all the while. The chief sat across from him, separated by a small banquet table. Crafted by the villagers, the chairs were surprisingly comfortable.

"Breakfast will be served in a moment. I am sure you are hungry after meeting the tenants of the mansion. I am also sure that you confided in this book most of the time." The chief reached under his seat and placed an ancient version of the bible on the table.

Because not many people owned them these days, Baelin sat up in his seat and said, "You can read, then?"

Crossing his legs, the chief began, "Sometime after the Primeval Tragedy, a doctor and his family came to that place. It was probably in ugly shape, so he and a team of supporters worked on making it more suitable to live in. You see, they were seeking a safer place to live at the time. It was common then for diseases to spread like wildfire. Well, this must have been one hell of a disease. They left the mainland to find refuge far away.

"They were doing fine for a while, until people started dying in their sleep. Suffocation was the diagnosis of their demise as the doctor saw it. They never could discover who was doing this, but many people started leaving the mansion. Well, that did not change anything. They found a servant dead in the atrium one morning, accompanied by a cracked lantern and nothing more. Some thought the plague made it into the safety of the house. That was foolishness, of course.

"One night, however, the maid saw something that would provide a horrific answer to the mad equation. Sarah Midvein, the doctor's very own daughter, was committing the murders. But, it wasn't really her, you see. She was but a ten-year-old girl. She suffered from a sickness that trounced all the medical journals. Little Sarah was possessed.

"She would snap out of it from time-to-time, but the demon was extremely powerful and had control over the girl. This demon found refuge here first and did not want any visitors. God knows how the evil spirit infiltrated the mansion in the first place. Regardless, the doctor turned to a priest from the outside to perform an exorcism on his daughter. It did not bode well.

"She killed him. She tore out the cleric's throat with her ten-year old teeth. A resident tried stabbing her to death as she slept one night, claiming that killing her was the only way to save everyone and, of course, free her soul. The doctor's brother-in-law stopped him just in time, but it brought a grim idea to light. If she died, the evil spirit would find another host until there was no one left. Only the worst possible evil would exploit a father's daughter for such cruelty.

"Seeing that this demon was far too powerful, the doctor was convinced that there was no saving his little girl. Sedating her, he carried her limp body into the basement and left her there in chains. They, as a family, locked the door from the outside and woefully left the mansion forever. Of course the poor girl awoke to the blackness of a dank dungeon, hurt and petrified until she eventually wasted away and died."

"My God!" Baelin clenched the armrest of his seat, unable to imagine the agony, "They just left that innocent girl there to die? Not even an animal deserves that, for God's sake!"

"Be that as it may, legend has it that when she did die, the demon left her body and possessed the house once more. The Midveins, on the other hand, gathered their resources and started a little outpost by the seashore. They lived here for a few years in misery until the doctor stopped writing." Chief Hared took a sip of hot tea.

"Writing what?" He asked, nearly losing his appetite for Chimera's breakfast.

The chief reached under his seat again and held an old bound book before him, saying, "When we first came here, I found this book with the bible hidden in a chest. It is Doctor Midvein's personal diary. In it, he explains everything I told you, including the exorcism of Sarah."

"That basement—that dungeon is the source." Baelin glared at the old diary, "Does it mention where the basement is located?"

Lobbing the aged book by Baelin's breakfast, the chief reached for the hot bread and declared, "Read it for yourself. I imagine that you will find what you are looking for."

Waving the book in his hands, Baelin glared, "This would have been helpful last night."

"Yes," The chief riposted without looking up, "it most certainly would have been."

Awkward pauses were becoming a habit for them. Baelin flipped through the old pages briefly before saying, "If there is something you are not telling me about that place, you are only hurting your own people."

Grinning scornfully from behind his dirty beard, the chief asked, "Is there anything else I can do for you, paladin?"

Baelin wiped his mouth and began to walk out of the dining room with the article in hand, speaking inertly, "Thank you for breakfast."

Observing Cletus escort the paladin out of the manor, the chief shouted so that he could hear from a distance, "I have nothing to hide! You are merely blinded by your virtues—and your sins!"

Baelin had heard similar accusations from many cynics during the past three years. He did not need to hear it here from a cagey chief of a drifter village. When he sought for answers, he received riddles instead. It did not sit well with him. The secretive village of Chimera was becoming a suspicious retreat. Baelin felt as if he was being punished for his crimes. The path to redemption was lonely and chastening.

Escorted by Cletus Crow, Baelin thought about his dilemma. They walked along a path leading towards the northern exit when the church came into view on their right, just beside the unoccupied schoolhouse. He prayed every day for forgiveness and strength. This day was no different. But, would the church in this place pass the holy test?

"Think I will pray first, Cletus." Baelin declared after saying nothing during the present walk.

Seeming disappointed in himself for not remembering the paladin's religious needs, Cletus muttered, "Oh, yes, of course."

There was nothing uncommon about the church. Small, white, and located in the center of the village, the Chimera church humbly welcomed Baelin. The paladin stepped inside the sanctuary to pray and quickly realized its simplicity. There Jesus Christ hung from the cross over a modest altar. A villager was sweeping the wood floor as he entered, refusing to look the outsider in the eyes. He took his time to pray for God's blessings as Cletus looked on from outside, crossing his arms.

When he was finished, Baelin walked out to join Cletus, asking, "Have you a priest?"

"Yes," he answered swiftly, "Father Tom is blessing the sick in their homes, no doubt. That was some storm last night, no?"

Noticing the fast change of topic, Baelin humored, "Sudden, yes. I could have done without it."

He also could have done without the ungainly exchanges from socially deprived villagers. As they continued to walk up the path, Baelin considered the lesser stable by the exit gate. A horse would save him the unnecessary legwork to-and-from the Midvein Mansion. It would also save him time.

"I could use a horse, Cletus." Baelin mentioned while slowing down by the stall.

"A horse?" Cletus teased, "Eager to race back to that comfy demon preserve?"

When Baelin lowered his head and clutched the wooden fence separating him from a small group of horses, Cletus anxiously cleared his throat. Looking over the idle horses, Baelin sighed and said, "Cletus, I just want to go home. That is all I have left, my home back in Ellium. My father, mother, sister, and everyone else moved there for me. Now I am abandoned here."

"Can't they come to live here?" Cletus asked.

Snickering from disgust, Baelin re-joined, "And leave them for the Blood Reapers? You must be crazy. Have you seen them, Cletus? Have you ever had the pleasure?"

"Well, no, not—" Cletus was stopped midsentence.

"I guessed not." Baelin continued, "Better that way."

Cletus joined him in watching the horses while saying, "I have heard many stories about them. They were a sadistic cult of witches and cannibals. But they have not been seen since—"

"Don't bother." Baelin cut him off again, "They are still around here and you know that. Without a leader, they have gone into hiding."

"You and that witch cleaned this island of them." Cletus tried his spirit, "You did what you had to do."

Baelin pushed himself from the fence and hissed, "I said don't, Cletus. That is enough."

Attempting to avoid another difficult hiatus, Cletus adjusted his hood and headed towards the stable, saying distantly, "I will fetch your horse. Please return her in good shape."

Baelin had fought with himself for three years, attempting to draw a line between his just and prejudiced actions. This was his cross to bear, a punishment well fitted for a seditious knight of God. He began to ponder then why the New Vatican would even relieve him of his banishment. This one act was not enough. He had to do more than follow earthly orders from a council of magistrates. Baelin remembered his pledge to himself and to God.

He whispered towards the sky, "Lord Jesus Christ, please help me to walk, for I am so tired."

Moments later...

The horse was reluctant to proceed towards the mansion, for she sensed the evil there. Nonetheless, Baelin was able to calm her down just enough to make it to the entrance gate. The crows were everywhere this time. Flapping their wings, the cawing birds ogled Baelin and his new companion as they entered the front yard. He tied her to a post designed for horses, giving her enough slack to move around the place. She was still very flustered, for any animal could feel it.

Inside Midvein Mansion, Baelin immediately opened the doctor's disturbing diary and searched the old text for clues. He sat upon the master bed and flipped through the pages, careful not to tear them. The penmanship was not easy to scrim through, but he made due. Retracing the family's footsteps, Baelin tore the mansion apart, room by room, for signs. Toys left by the family drifted in the hallway as if they were underwater. He batted them away as he passed, not surprised by the poltergeists' scare tactics anymore. Eventually, he made it to the first floor where the final events of the exorcism took place.

Baelin threw desks and chairs out of the way, breaking them against the walls. He kicked over couches and shelves, looking for secret doorways to the dungeon. The only real clue the diary left entailed the storage room. The doctor wrote that he, "...felt the chill of the basement inside the storeroom ..."

Opening the rickety door, Baelin instantly felt a faint burst of cool air run through his hair and tingle his senses. An eerie whisper resounded within before fading away, serving more as a welcome than a warning now. Baelin retrieved the Divine Mace from upstairs and illuminated the storage room. The artificial lights had not worked for six hundred years. Stepping inside, he could already feel the dampness of the Midvein basement.

This place was unholy indeed. Cackling and crying sprung up from the shadows of the room, testing his resolve. The chill was uncomfortably wet on his skin. Wraithlike chants turned up and enveloped the chamber, becoming louder with every verse. These dark voices incessantly chanted, "The dead are forgotten!"

Despite his angst, Baelin proceeded to walk deeper into the storage room, looking for an entrance to the basement. He kicked over shelves and old, moldy boxes of scrap before noticing a strange carving in the decaying wallpaper. A portion of the paper was sodden and spoilt, revealing slabs of brick behind it.

Likely done by a knife, the etching said, "You will burn!"

Baelin had seen this before, only it was written in blood on the doctor's chamber door. It ran chills up his spine. The chanting stopped, permitting the paladin to tear away the decrepit wallpaper in stillness. Doing so, he realized that the paper had been torn from the wall once before. Someone meddled with the old paper, pasting it back onto the moistened wall of brick.

Having to uncover the hidden door to the basement, Baelin heatedly stripped the paper away and, at last, sealed his doom. There was another carving in the slab. He recognized it right away, as the deep agony of the curse began to infiltrate his body. Baelin jerked away quickly and dropped the Divine Mace to the floor, grunting from the intense pain that tore through his veins.

It was a fully detailed curse, a hex made especially for trespassers. It was in the form of a satanic pentagram, with the skull of a goat prying dissonantly into the soul. Six colorful runes of destruction enveloped the engraving, empowering the hex. This was a superior form of black magic. Victims under this spell suffered an agonizing death, as the body attacked itself from within. The average person was set to die in a day's time.

Baelin fell to the ground and held out his right arm, for it was with his right hand that he touched the spell. He looked up at it with trepidation as he fought to stay awake. While writhing on the floor, he shut his eyes and prayed to God for strength. The lonely paladin moaned from a dazing pain in the oppression of darkness, knowing that he had to gain control over the curse fast.

Powerful paladins, while invulnerable to most magic, could only suppress such curses for so long. Baelin temporarily stifled the spell within minutes, having faith in his holy abilities. It was not gone, but dormant. Judging by the ferocity of it, Baelin estimated that he had three days before it eventually overtook him for good. Any typical man would have been dead by sunset.

He could not cure this ghastly spell on his own. Because a dealer of the dark arts dealt the curse, only another sorcerer of equal or greater talents could reverse it. Baelin rose to his knees and panted, sweating from the taxing ordeal. He knew of only one person who could save him now. She was the Witch of Swamp Hill.

Taking a knapsack, Baelin carried his mace and some food rations for the desperate journey. He stumbled out of the mansion and spit out some regurgitated blood from his mouth. The crows flew away sporadically, for they sensed the curse on him. The Chimera horse was no different. The wounded paladin mounted the steed and raced for the forests to the northeast.

There was no time to decipher how and why the evil spell was put to the wall. Baelin could deal with that after he found a cure. That is, if he could find the elusive witch. Her reputation was of the dark kind, but they shared a common trait. The Blood Reapers feared them. In fact, her influence over the cult made her a living legend. Yet, she was no friend to the paladin. Even if he could find her, Baelin could only hope that she would have pity. His very life was at stake and time was running out.

Redeem the Knight
Mercy VI

Two years ago…

Following the chastening trial within the Paladin's Sanctum, Arl bid his goodbyes. To his family, friends, and brothers-in-arms, he expressed regret for the abrupt fall from grace. For the rest of his life, Arl was to live in exile in Islandia. And because he was deemed worthy of perpetuating the paladin title, he was to become the island's official holy knight. However, the elders warned him that one more transgression meant his expulsion from the order and a prolonged prison sentence.

Arl's return to Islandia merited mixed salutations. While some favored him, many others viewed him as the fallen knight who betrayed them. Alone and without the support of Babylonia, the island's first city, Arl became a wandering soul in search of redemption. Not surprisingly, he received no orders from the New Vatican. If losing his family, wife, and child was not enough, the Blood Reapers sought him out to finish the chore.

While he battled the leaderless sect of deviants, the corpses of secret Blood Reaper affiliates wound up all over the island. Politicians and peasants alike were being murdered. Under investigation, it was clear that each victim had traceable ties to the Blood Reapers. Arl was attributed to the killings at first, but further scrutiny proved his innocence in most cases.

Soon, talk of a mysterious witch from the swamps surfaced. She was merciless in her killings of the reapers, or any who got in her way. The Witch of Swamp Hill, as she was called, had a small army of followers that did her bidding in nasty ways. When bodies started to turn up around cities and towns, it was evident that not all of the fatalities were of Blood Reaper affiliation. So,

Arl Baelin took the charge to find this witch and put an end to her haphazard butcheries.

Since the deaths of Gideon and Alec, the gypsies allegedly cleared out of Swamp Hill, deeming it unsafe. Arl trekked there, risking the painful memories that could stir up, and called out for the cryptic sorceress to show herself. Rumors spread about those who entered Swamp Hill to find her and never returned. Arl was not afraid. There was so little to lose now.

Wielding the Divine Mace, he ambled deeper into the familiar swamplands. In moments, swarms of aggressors emerged from the cover of brush to curse and challenge him. After a brief scuffle, a woman cried out and the assailants winced back. They made a path for him to follow so that he may finally meet their leader. Her minions wore makeup so that they would not be easily recognizable. It worked.

From atop a memorable boulder, the notorious witch revealed herself. She was adorned in a purple gown and bejeweled in the spoils of her reaper conquests. Crude daggers hung snuggly from her midriff and her pale smooth legs refused to be suppressed by the decadence of clothing. Wearing dark boots that matched the color of her lips, the Witch of Swamp Hill glared down the paladin intruder.

She put her mystical staff to the side and proclaimed, "Arl Baelin, welcome back to Swamp Hill."

Arl was certain that it was another tantalizing dream stalking his spirit. Seeing the witch triggered so many emotions. It weakened him—damaged his focus. Flashing images of his wife conquered his mind. However, as sudden as the illusions of Gideon appeared, the reality hit him like a spear through the heart. The Witch of Swamp Hill was no stranger of happenstance.

"Oh God!" Arl gasped after looking her over, "Gideon?"

"Swamp Hill has changed since you have seen me last," she replied icily, "and so have I."

Arl, stunned by the pitiless realism, stumbled forward and exclaimed, "I thought you were dead! I thought they killed you!"

Gideon censured him from atop her boulder, extending her index finger like a baron, "Stay where you are! The Gideon you knew is dead! She was too weak to withstand the torment alone."

Because he was still so shocked, Arl was hardly able to register what she had said. No mother could ever return to her previous life after losing a child. Gideon, though suspected dead, was not the same woman as the year before. When he realized that she was not right, he stopped dead in his tracks.

"Gideon, what happened to you? Why did you not come to find me? You killed hordes of reapers all over the island, but let me wander alone without a family — without knowing if you were alive or dead?" Arl cried out in disbelief, "I know what they did to Alec! I know what they did to you!"

"Shut up!" She screamed in return, "You were not there, so don't pretend you know anything!"

Clenching his fist, Arl fired back, "I was there with you! They struck at me first! They knew about us."

"I told you what I would do if they hurt us!" Gideon's eyes started to tear in her rage, "I told you!"

There the guilt hit him. He tried so many nights to convince her that they were protected from the evils of the outside world. He tried so many times that he ultimately swayed her worried soul. Because she loved him so, Gideon trusted his word. His word was not enough to save them. Bowing his head, Arl uttered, "I know."

With her followers surrounding the paladin, Gideon proclaimed, "So, you have come to stop me? You have returned here only to stifle the vengeance that is rightfully mine to take? You will not!"

"For God's sake, it's only a matter of time before they find you a second time! When you go too far, all of Islandia will come for you, too, and you know that! Is that what you want? Do you wish to bring more death to these people?" Arl called up at her.

"More death?" Taken aback by his sentiments, she said, "You have the nerve to make me the villain? No, I will do as I promised, now that your hollow dreams of denial have ended! If you intend on stopping me, you will have to kill me."

Arl moved steps closer in his distress, shouting desperately, "Gideon, damn you! It does not have to happen this way! Just talk to me! Talk to me as the woman I love – as my wife!"

She threw her staff down to a receiving disciple and shouted, "You are not listening! That woman is dead!"

"Our son is dead!" He cried in return, "I cry day and night for him still to this day. I have the blood of those responsible on my hands. Stop while you can, before you cannot wash the blood off at all. You are still alive, Gideon! Please come back to me. Come back to real life."

Seeming desensitized, Gideon jumped down from the boulder and slowly advanced for him, showing off her hands in the process, "We both have blood on our hands – Alec's. We bore him into a world that was bound to destroy him."

Arl dropped the Divine Mace and kicked it behind him, replying with tension, "I have lost my son. Do not expect me to walk away from my wife. We are – "

Gideon questionably placed her hands behind her back as she came closer to interrupt him, saying, "But I am not your wife anymore. Your naïve courage aided in her demise."

When she was only feet away from him, Arl shut his eyes in despair, "Gideon, my heart cannot take much more of this. Everything I have ever loved has been taken from me."

"Can't you see as I do?" She said to him, "No more shall I be merciful to those who stand against me. That includes you, a false hero without purpose. I have an army of brothers and sisters who believe in the cause. Who do you have—God? Look at what He has allowed to happen! You are forsaken. Can't you see?"

Thoughts of his influences on the world made him sick, yet a voice within demanded that he remember who he was and who he could become again. Arl still had family in Ellium that loved and prayed for him. He had close friends that had not betrayed his trust. Islandics still opened their arms to him in thankfulness for the blessings he bestowed upon them times before. While many forsook him, those who were dearest to him never forgot his brave acts of kindness.

Clearly, the horror that occurred in this place a year ago had left Gideon alive, but dead inside. Only hatred and shame remained, leading her to kill in order to forget. Her strength and magnificence soured into cold vengeance, for that was the new motivation. Gideon traded faith for fear.

Believing that God promised redemption, Arl lifted his sulking head and boldly replied, "Can't you see as I do? I was selfish in thinking that I could have you and be a paladin at the same time, but I do not regret our love for each other. God did not punish us. Only in the eyes of this world was our love forbidden. I believe that redemption is possible and I will seek it out for what I have done. As for you, I will offer one last chance to surrender this bloody campaign. I do not wish to hurt you."

Nearing in dangerously close to his face, she let one hand from behind her back and caressed his lips, saying woefully, "But, my darling, you already have."

In a sudden move, Gideon brought her other hand around to slit his throat with an unsheathed dagger. The blade barely cut through his skin, for Arl pulled away just in time. She spun about to unsheathe the other crude dagger from her waste and attempted to stab him in the neck. He seized Gideon's wrist, pushed her away, and then went to retrieve his mace. When a gypsy tried to take it first, Arl kicked him in the face and rolled on the ground, snatching it as he rose to his feet.

Gideon was sure not to fight him with magic alone, for she knew that true paladins were resistant to most spells. The witch, instead, hurled one of her blades for his chest. The knife cast was accurate, but Arl batted it away with his mace. She then tried an incantation, chanting a spell that weighed his legs. Feeling to fall, Arl collapsed to his knee and used the mace as leverage to prevent his drop. Gideon ran to finish him right there.

It was not nearly enough to keep Arl vulnerable to the kill. He broke free from the casting and held up his Divine Mace in defense of the oncoming assault. She drove the knife down, though he caught it with the shaft of his holy weapon, deflecting it to the side and striking her in the face with one swift move. Gideon was accustomed to pain and his hit was nothing. Arl repositioned himself again to defend the next attack.

Another incantation. She twirled her arms around her and released a casting that burned his eyes from within, compelling him to shut them. Unexpectedly, a bold gypsy woman retrieved one of Gideon's knives and came from behind the paladin to stab him in the back. While laboring to see, Arl sensed the surprise attack and tried to thwart it. Nonetheless, she plunged the blade into the weakness of his armor, just making it through his flesh.

He let out a brief cry before elbowing her over his shoulder and then following through with a fierce kick to the stomach. She collided into the dense group of gypsies, dropping the dagger as she fell. Wounded, Arl stared down the throng with daggers of his own. In the angry heat of conflict, Gideon cried out from a distance, "No, he is mine! This is my fight!"

Hearing this, Arl stood up straight, despite his stamina, and shouted passionately, "I won't fight you any longer! If you wish to have your vengeance, then take it now! Kill me here where I stand and come full circle!"

She watched him stand there in submission, captivating her to kill him. As she charged for him, screaming all the way, Gideon was hurt. Her heart did not want this. Yet, she gripped the dagger in her hand with conviction and went to slice his throat like before. All the while, Arl just stood there.

Once she had him, she cried louder and brought the blade to his neck. As her followers looked on in awe, she held the knife up to his sweaty throat and let it stay there. Arl still stood there just the same, unflinchingly, and looked into her harrowing eyes. Of all the anger and shame she felt, Gideon could not bring herself to kill him. Even though she blamed him for so many things that had happened to her and their son, Gideon simply could not make the ultimate fault and murder the man she loved for so long.

In her eyes, Arl could finally see the anguish firsthand. Her soul was broken and there was no way for him to repair it. In the end, he could not keep his promises to the people he dearly loved. Because there was nothing else that he could do, Arl slowly backed away and cried. He let the tears run down his face. Gideon, in return, did the same.

Overcome by sadness and guilt, the forlorn paladin left Swamp Hill. He took the displaced dagger and walked through the throng of Gideon's people unhindered. On that day, he vowed that he would never return to Swamp Hill. On that day, his spirit had taken a blow, for which he would never forget.

Now in Swamp Hill, two years later…

For the sake of his own life and the mission, Baelin had no choice but to break his vow and return to Swamp Hill. He rode feebly on the Chimera horse, hunched over and breathing with careful composure. He finished a few snacks on the way to keep his body nourished for the journey. There was no telling if Gideon still hid there. This was a chance of desperation.

The place had not changed much since he had been there last. The memories were not welcoming. Human skulls stuck on polls as he rode deeper into the notorious swamp, serving as a reminder of what happened to those who wandered too far. The warning was a good omen. Perhaps she was still there.

Baelin's veins were tingling numb from the curse. Feeling like he was going to faint, he fell off the horse and landed on his back. As the satchel flopped to the side, the paladin rose to his knees and shouted amidst the lingering fog, "Gideon!"

The fraught cry was his last surge of energy, for he was physically exhausted. The sky turned to night in moments and his eyes rolled back into his head. It was better for a paladin to stay awake while battling poisons and curses, but Baelin could not stand it. He trusted in God for protection as he blacked out.

As if the world was moving under him, Baelin felt like he was in-between life and death. Collectively, hands lifted him off the ground and carried his body above the marshy soil. No longer did he feel cold. The tingling stopped and he felt at peace. Yet, the warm feeling he had not felt in years did not last long. A voice was bothersome, calling out to him, "Paladin, wake up!"

Eventually, the tingling returned, as did the pain. Baelin's world was spinning again when his eyes opened to see the boundless night sky. Stars glittered above, amassing around the bright crescent moon. Soon enough, he realized that a gypsy tended to him, wetting his forehead and serving water. Another familiar face passed by in the dark, sneezing as he walked by. And there next to him, a unique woman had come into focus.

Though he tried to say her name, Gideon spoke over him, "That horse you rode in on—it is ours now."

Clearing his throat, he declared, "I could use your help."

"You're a brave fool." Gideon griped, "I do not know where you have been creeping, but a great curse has taken you over. However, you will not accept death, will you? No, you are much too stubborn for that sort of business."

"I promised myself that I would never come back here again, but I had no choice." Baelin said from the ground, "You're the only one I know that could reverse this scourge."

"You are lucky, Baelin." She replied with a sinister smile, "The only reason I am intrigued to help you is so that I may learn more about this captivating spell. I have never seen anything quite like it. Where did you catch this cold, I wonder?"

"Midvein Mansion." He peered deeper into her eyes, "I was very close to solving its ghost predicament when this sprung up on me. It looked newer than anything else in that place."

Gideon took a moment before sending her minions away. She wanted to be alone with him by the fire. The gypsies watched him from afar, always looking to protect their sorceress. The fire behind Gideon made her into a partial silhouette as she stood over the lone paladin. It was evident now that the New Vatican had found a use for him again, or he would not have ventured into such a dark site.

When Baelin moved onto his knee, she placed her hands on her hips and asked, "How did you know that I was still here?"

"A small measure of faith." Baelin retorted from his knee.

Shaking her head, she said, "Well, it will take more than your 'faith' to survive this one cleanly. How far is the source of the hex from here? I need to see it in order for me to reverse it."

"A few miles or more. I don't know right now." He covered his eyes in an attempt to avert the vertigo.

Scheming over his bent frame, Gideon sighed and said, "You have slept for hours, so it is too late for us to head out now. First thing tomorrow, you will lead me to this mansion and our covenant will end there. It would be a shame for you to die in your sleep, so please channel all your healing."

Whilst she began walking away from him, he snickered towards the crackling fire, "I see you have not lost your charm."

Irked, Gideon turned back and kicked him in the face. After he fell to the ground, she slumped over him and hissed, "Do not become comfortable here, Baelin. At dawn, we are strangers, you understand me? I could care less about you or your self-righteous pursuits. Reversing that curse upon you will teach me how to use it for myself. After that, we are done. Come back here one more time and it will be your skull on that pole!"

Even as he believed her candid threat, Baelin felt that there was still a piece of the real Gideon somewhere inside that shell of hatred and shame. He never learned her perspective of what happened on that horrid night that changed everything. Now she seemed distant, but closer than the last time. It was strange. She coerced herself into forgetting him, though her soul could not flourish without his love.

They took him by the arms and tossed his limp body into a small moss hut. Gypsies that remembered him during the good days offered jugs of water and baskets of food for sustenance. The last one lit two candles before leaving. Baelin rested on his back and breathed methodically, meditating and channeling his healing influences. She confiscated his mace, and for good reason. The Divine Mace was to a paladin as the fishing pole was to an angler.

Baelin only had to survive the night to be saved. In the morning, Gideon would inspect the hex and learn how to reverse the evil spell cast upon him. He was confident in that. As for now, he had to surrender himself to God. Even in this dark evening of strife, Baelin believed that heaven would enhance his strength. This quest of cleansing a haunted mansion was quickly turning into a quest to cleanse his very self.

After morning…

It was the second night without a good sleep. His body stung from inside and his skin was hot. Baelin woke up to a warm breakfast, though not to a warm reception. Gideon tossed him his satchel holding the Divine Mace and told him to hurry, for they were to set out in a moment's time. She foresaw that the weather was going to be gloomy for the entire day: a bad omen.

On the same horse Baelin rode in on, Gideon rode out towards Midvein Mansion. He grappled her from behind to keep balance, which felt good, but tore up his soul. The last time he held her this way, they were lovers. The horse's galloping did not help his composure. Baelin closed his eyes and just meditated on his strength.

It shocked him of how little she wished to converse. He was not in the mood to banter much anyway, but even a smile from her would have lifted his spirits. There was no time to worry about personal matters, for they had already arrived at the haunted mansion. The ominous overcast fit the atmosphere inside that place. Once Gideon reached the site, it was evident that her direction was true.

When Baelin noticed that they arrived so quickly, he grunted from behind her, "How did you know where it was?"

"When were you going to tell me?" She replied as the nervous horse neared closer to the ancient house, "Clairvoyance. This mansion of yours emits a baleful power. I cannot understand how I did not notice its presence earlier."

Looking at the mansion as if it was returning his gaze, Baelin said jadedly, "It hid from all of us."

She steered the horse carefully into the gate, enduring stares from vagrant crows. They welcomed the next victim of Midvein Mansion with caws. Gideon helped him off the horse and they ventured into the house. Once they did, the spooked Chimera horse bolted from the gate and ran off into the mist. As they watched the steed fade away, Baelin coughed, "You don't ride horses often, do you?"

Gideon shook her head and realized what she was risking by helping him. Though she could not see them, a multitude of restless spirits ambled about the house. There was a clear presence of evil everywhere. When she clinched her free hand in angst, Baelin pointed Gideon in the proper direction of the basement. She wasted no time in helping the feeble paladin stumble for the dark corridor.

Upon entering, Baelin brought the satchel down from his back and tried to take out his mace to shed some light. Gideon opened her hand and ignited a small orb of purple radiance that hovered just above her palm. Nevertheless, he let the satchel fall and held the mace tightly, knowing that the curse was just ahead. By this time, the feeling was strong. She knew where it was.

"Lay here." She let him down and inspected the elaborate curse for herself, saying with apprehension, "I have never seen any spell like this before. It is deviously sophisticated."

"I'm glad you like it." He moaned.

Chanting a mantra, Gideon held her hands out towards the curse and illuminated the room with a bright yellow charge of magic. An expert in her craft, she absorbed the sinister properties of the hex within an instant. Her eyes lit up the same color and she smiled, understanding the complexities of it all.

However, when the incantation was finished, a brief image of the curse's master appeared in her mind. She had never seen such a sorcerer before, but it frightened her. He wore a black cloak and wielded a scythe. He emulated the grim reaper well, though she could not make out his face. It was then that she appreciated the caster even more. This curse was far too complex for her to attempt. While she understood its workings, Gideon feared that its misuse could kill her.

"Well?" Baelin pleaded from his back, "What happened?"

Shaken, she asked him, "So, another enemy to notch onto the belt? Do you even know what you are doing in this place?"

"Who did you see?" He said while holding his forehead.

Seeing that he was in writhing agony, Gideon swallowed her pride and groaned. She could not successfully acquire the curse fully, but she could potentially reverse the spell's effect on him. The mystical code was not easy to undo, for it could kill him in the process. Of course, Gideon was not about to tell him that, even if witnessing him cringe in fear would have been lovely.

"Lie still." The witch covered his forehead with her right hand glowing yellow from the spell. As she worked on him, Baelin's hold on the mace's handle became tighter. It was painful to stop the curse midstream, for the mysterious spell was resisting. Even so, the mace's head illuminated a livelier blue as the reversing spell carried on.

The possessed mansion did not approve of the paladin's healing. It made the spirits agitated, engendering a sinister aura about them. Gideon shut her eyes and proceeded with the exhausting spell regardless of the haunting sensations that assailed her nerve. Soon enough, the light of the mace shined brighter and Baelin was breathing easier. When Gideon removed her hand and held her own wrist in fatigue, Baelin's natural healing abilities had taken over. Gideon had cured him.

They remained silent in the corridor, catching their breaths. Gideon concluded her journey empty handed as Baelin lie healed. Gaining strength with every heartbeat, the paladin controlled his breathing and moved to his knee. Gideon looked him over with bitter eyes, expecting a reward for her contribution to his holy quest. He returned her gaze and nodded his head in gratitude.

Still, there was the main event of his mission left to carry out before the day was done. Now that the curse was stripped of its power, Baelin was able to pass through into the beckoning mystery of the subterranean vault. Because she did not tie the horse to anything, Gideon was compelled to stay with him and learn the truth behind Midvein Mansion's terrible haunting. Baelin was sure that the source to the demonic inhabitants' power rested within. He held the Divine Mace with both hands and looked into his soul for calmness. Only God knew what waited for him.

Redeem the Knight
Penance VII

One year ago...

Within the empty halls of Saint Lena's Cathedral in Babylonia, Arl Baelin had met with the bishop in private. Early morning on every other Saturday, the New Vatican sent envelopes of money to their paladins so they may use it for all sorts of holy purposes. As any man, a holy knight needs to eat, sleep, and pray under shelter. So, too, then does this man need to use the money to feed the hungry, provide for the poor, and clothe the naked.

In a few moments, the cathedral of Islandia's capital would open once again for public service. They waited outside, knowing that their paladin was finishing up with the bishop and needed time alone to talk and receive proper blessings. Because Babylonia was a center of learning, many debates sprouted from Arl's exile from Ellium. The waiting crowds outside had different stances on this troubling issue.

He received the bishop's faithful sacrament along with the envelope gorging with monies. Upon leaving the cathedral through the front doors, the fully armored paladin nodded his head to the masses, ready to help the needy. As most passed by to enter the place of worship, some stayed back and beseeched their hero for blessings, alms, and healing. In his heart, Arl no longer felt worthy of the healing task. He had taken his penance so far as to remove the blood ring from his finger.

Arl carried a satchel on his back, containing the bible and Divine Mace. He left his valise in the trust of his good friend, Ronald Tumbler in Linden. Nonetheless, he still possessed the will to provide for his people as their paladin. Yet, as he prepared to bless the crowd, an armed man stood in the square with dueling blades in his hands. Looking like an assassin, people moved away from him so that Arl Baelin could see him clearly.

"Receive no blessing from that anti-Christ," said the man, "for he is nothing but a killer and a coward!"

Arl scrutinized the man carefully from the bottom steps of the cathedral. He had shaggy hair and wore tightfitting clothes. The empty sheathes on his back proved that he came to kill, not to talk. The blades were black and sharp as razors. This was not just a mere assassin, for he did not try to take his life in stealth. This man wanted Arl to know his slayer. This was personal.

Arl gazed over the masses and said, "If you have come here looking for a fight, you have come to the wrong place. These people are in need of peace, not blood. Leave."

"I will not leave without your head!" The man cried out, shocking the crowd.

Arl signaled for his people to make way, countering, "If you have come all this way to Babylonia's cathedral to kill me, then you must have a good reason to die."

"I come for my father!" The man shouted, raising a blade, "You, like a coward, murdered him in the dead of night and let his body rot by the fire! You suspected him to be a Blood Reaper, but he was a vexed man who did what he could to feed his sons! If you were a paladin, as these fools believe you to be, then you would have heard him and learned that he was a man with a broken mind and a heart full of guilt!"

At that moment, Arl realized that his past actions had come to haunt him. City guards began to surround the man with swords drawn, but waited for the paladin to act in response. Lowering his head first, Arl replied with regret in his voice, "I have committed my fair share of sins, and for that I seek redemption. I ask for your forgiveness for what I have done."

"Forgiveness?" He gasped, "You must think me mad if I will accept your forgiveness and walk away as if nothing ever happened! I will ask for your blood!"

"You cannot have it." Arl rejoined, "Do not make my mistakes in thinking that blood washes away blood."

The man, clearly offended, laughed and then proclaimed, "This comes from a man who murdered any who challenged him in his turn of rage fit for a jackal! What a hoax! Your crimes merited banishment to Islandia, our home, as if it were a just punishment! You killed the Witch of Swamp Hill like a hired hand and we are to say 'thank you' for your good graces? Never! I challenge you to a duel, here and now, for the life of my father! What do you say to that?"

By the look in his eyes, Arl understood that this was not just a measly challenge for the sake of vengeance. This man burned inside much as he did two years ago. This was an angry duel of honor and Arl could have denied him, but he did not. He nodded and ambled through the clearing crowd to meet him in the square.

"So be it." Arl replied amongst his stunned sympathizers, "I will accept your challenge, but not here. I ask that we take this to the field up there, away from the cathedral."

The man agreed and followed the paladin up the incline and onto the grassy field in the supervision of Babylonian soldiers. Spectators were not far behind them as one guard offered Arl his sword. He received it and asked that they keep the onlookers a fair distance away. Without saying much of anything, the soldiers acknowledged the duel and prevented the witnesses from wandering deeper into contest territory.

Arl placed his satchel onto the grass and loosened up, playing with the blade in his hand. As the crowd turned into a dazed mob, the man twirled his swords and positioned himself twenty paces opposite his enemy. Staring him down with daggers, the man proclaimed, "I could have murdered you as you slept, but I shall break the cycle of dishonor that you started. I trained and lost so much to prepare for this very moment. Finally, you die."

Arl wished to redeem himself for past transgressions, but forgiveness not given led to this. Words were not going to ease the stranger's storm that bellowed in his heart. His storm served as a replacement drive for aspirations. Though he saw his enemy before him, the vengeful assassin could not see his senseless sacrifices of loved ones and dreams once sought after.

"Let us be done with this." Arl said, steadying the blade.

Immediately, the man charged for the paladin with blades spread out towards the horizon. Arl took a defensive stance and deflected the oncoming strikes with a single sword. They clanged blades before the crowd, leaving them all in suspenseful anxiety. Finding an opening, Arl evaded a hack and countered with a pommel to the chin. The man winced back, spit, and then returned to battle.

He could feel the anger in the man's relentless blows rattling off the blade. The clanking sounds echoed about the field as they fought. Arl received a slash to the arm and then another to his waist, bearing bloody reparation for his sins. Soon after another matched bout, he let the man cut his thigh and then just pierce his lower back. While his opponent reveled in his success, Arl looked to the heavens and offered his wounding as repentance.

But his plea for forgiveness put him off-guard, for the vengeful man held no other desire than the paladin's ruin. He fought on angrily until Arl became overwhelmed by the flurry. As the masses gasped in alarm and awe, the assassin slashed the paladin's throat with a horizontal spinning hack. It would have most certainly sliced off his head, but Arl was able to pull away in time. The angry lesion spewed a steady stream of blood from the side of his neck.

Arl put pressure on his throat and fell to his knee, keeping an unyielding eye on his adversary. Without any hesitation, the unforgiving avenger rushed his prey to finish off what he had started. In a swift movement, he dashed with gnashing teeth to slice off his head just as he had promised. However, the paladin was not prepared to offer his life just yet.

Instead of his life, Arl offered a stunning counter maneuver. Using the guard's sword, he deflected both blades and gored his foe's abdomen from his knee. The strike was adeptly quick as it was deadly, for the sword ran deep. The onlookers shouted and then hushed within seconds. Though most of the crowd approved of the outcome with gaping eyes, Arl regarded his opponent. He removed the bloody sword and let the defeated man rest on his back, confounded and hurting.

Just when he thought that the paladin was finished, he was beaten. His eyes revealed the glossy anguish of his failure to avenge his father. Arl could have kneeled and recited the man's last rite, but he chose differently. He tore open the man's blouse and assessed the gaping wound. Covering it with his own bloody hand, the paladin channeled his remorse.

Arl said to him, "You have taken my blood with honor, but you cannot take my life. I must redeem myself for dire sins of vengeance. Yet, you have almost repeated my sins this day. You say that you have lost so much in your quest to avenge your father, but forsake your family and your very soul in the process.

"Be the man that I should have been. Turn your life around and seek God's high counsel, for my death will not heal you. Only one who seeks forgiveness of sins and practices righteous work can do these things. May your heavy heart heal as well as your flesh."

When Arl had finished with him, the paladin rose up and tended to his own wounds. Still lying in the grass, the man watched as his adversary started to leave the battleground. Yet, before he could rise up and resume the duel, he looked to his abdominal lesion. Amazed, he wiped the blood from the skin and admired the work of the paladin. Arl Baelin healed the mortal wound completely.

Upon touching and prodding his flesh to find where the gash had been, the vengeful man remained on the soil and suddenly lost his lust for settling scores. Arl, walking towards the gawking bystanders, retrieved his satchel and returned to the people in need. He cleaned the sword before placing it back into the hands of the guard that offered it, asking that the fallen duelist be permitted to leave Babylonia without harm.

In Midvein Mansion, one year later…

The door fell in upon itself from Baelin's kick, delivering a dank rush of putrid odors. The basement's rank keep was a sign of what lingered in the moistened dark below. However, the greatest warning stood behind them, as Gideon felt a chill run up her spine. She looked over her shoulder and then tugged on Baelin's armor.

There inside the room, apparitions assembled in silence to witness them descend into the bowels of the mansion. They stood in throngs, just watching. Baelin kept the illuminated mace close in the process, returning their gaze. The opening of the tomb of sorts was a milestone in the mansion's dismal course. While Gideon was unsure how to respond, Baelin's first instinct was to start down the clammy steps.

"Are you coming?" He asked from inside the stairway.

"I have company." Gideon said, "Happy tomb raiding."

Proceeding down the stairs, he mumbled, "Fair enough."

The smell was progressively potent as he made his way into the basement. Soon enough, Baelin found himself stepping into stagnant water. The sinking foundation flooded the lower level of the house, turning it into a virtual bog. Swimming rats and various insects scampered about as he trudged through, looking for the remains of Sarah Midvein.

Trampling over junk and rodents, Baelin covered his mouth and headed for the furnace and plumbing. His instincts were rewarded as an old chain ran stringently from a crude pipe into the murky water. After taking a closer look, the glow of the mace revealed a small skeleton frame. Sarah's black hair floated to the surface and her hand remained shackled.

The pipe was worn from the force of a young girl trying to pull herself free. Seeing her skeletal remains clenched his heart. It was bad enough that he had to hear of this tale, let alone see her for himself. Feeling as if he was being watched from the darkness of the flooded dungeon, Baelin propped up Sarah's body against the wall and started wailing on the decrepit pipe.

After four loud resounding strikes from his mace, Baelin mangled Sarah's prison and carried her soaking bones in his arms. He coughed from the smell, though it stemmed more from the prolonged effects of the curse than anything else. His visit to the source of Midvein's haunting was an unpleasant one. A terrible feeling struck him, as he had expected.

As he scaled the stairs, Gideon's hazy silhouette waited at the top. He could not resist beholding Sarah's face and imagining how fair it must have looked once. Now, centuries later, it was a miracle that her bones remained whole. Baelin mourned for the girl. It was not her choice to become possessed or to die. Her entire life seemed scourged.

Covering her nose, Gideon blurted, "This is your source?"

Baelin passed her and continued through the uninhabited storeroom. The converging spirits had left the room once he released Sarah from her undeserving bondage. Scrutinizing him carry the dripping remains of a girl out towards the atrium, Gideon asked where he was going. He said nothing. On impulse, she ran after him and asked louder, "Where are you going with that?"

Heading for the main doors, he answered, "I am going to give her a proper burial."

Over an hour later...

The brittle shovel finally broke after all the digging and covering out in the yellow fields. Five hundred feet out of the sight of the accursed mansion, Baelin buried Sarah's body and fashioned a wooden cross with her name etched on it. He prayed for her soul and provided compassion hundreds of years overdue.

Pleased that she could rest, as any child of God was entitled, Baelin gathered the weary tools and planned to return them to the mansion's frail toolshed. He left his personal things with Gideon, excluding his mace. Only now did he regret such a decision. She still could not be trusted, even with saving his life. Nevertheless, Gideon, the Blood Reapers, and even his quest for redemption had to be put aside, for his final task lay before him.

A last rite of cleansing within the basement was all that stood in the way of his mission's end. Baelin could see it unfold in his head. He would retrieve his mace along with the holy things in his case and eliminate the demonic presence inside Midvein Mansion, redeeming his title as a true paladin. Yet, it would take more than an overlooked haunted house to set the holy light of the Paladin's Sanctum back upon him.

While pondering these things, Baelin made it back to the mansion and saw four figures waiting at the main gate. Nearing closer, he realized that they were not vagabonds. Vigilantly, he dropped his things and kept his distance. They did not seem the peaceful type and Gideon was nowhere to be seen. He did not like this surprise one bit.

Clenching his fists, Baelin declared, "What business do you have here?"

"You are our business, Baelin." One of them said, "We have come to kill you."

"Only four of you?" He returned, unafraid.

The masked one in the back replied, "Yes. We are the four missing villagers of Chimera in the flesh."

A knot pulled his stomach. For sure, he must have been lying. He saw the graves for himself in Chimera village. The men unsheathed their blades and clubs to defeat him as a unit. Their attire of frayed leather and blood sodden cloth lit a candle in his mind. They were Blood Reaper extremists. Most of them vanished after Gideon's relentless purge. But why would they claim to be the lost villagers?

The same reaper said, "And when we are done with you, we shall devour your blood along with your tired soul."

Losing all guilt in the event of killing them, Baelin cracked his knuckles and proclaimed, "Let's get to work."

Three of them dashed for him at once in the hopes of a quick kill. Baelin kicked up the Divine Mace and caught it in his right hand, evening the odds. The reaper most eager for Baelin's head met his end in seconds, for the paladin deflected the first strike of the blade back into the owner's throat by way of the mace. He collapsed to the ground and murmured his last curse in the reddened dirt.

The next two tried him, but Baelin parried their blows and pulled away from the battle. In defense, he held his mace before him, unwaveringly. One reaper carelessly stepped on his own comrade's corpse to close in on the paladin. The other crept behind him, hoping to make him anxious enough to make a mistake. The fourth simply watched them behind the mask. Baelin kept his composure and timed his opponent's advance with trained prudence.

While the reaper before him threatened to attack, it was his enemy in behind that struck. Baelin hurriedly turned about to block the sword with his mace before landing a square punch to the side of the jaw. As the attacker winced back, the other came in to impale him in his side. Just barely evading the devastating thrust, Baelin snagged his arm and broke it at the elbow.

The reaper dropped the blade and shouted out in agony, but then smiled deviously right after. His teeth were red, as if he was eating raw flesh just moments ago. Fearing for Gideon's life, Baelin pushed him away and picked up the short sword from the dirt. Enraged by their vain bloodlust, he leaped with mace in hand and came down with a crushing blow to the skull.

After his second foe fell lifelessly onto his back, Baelin looked over his shoulder to size up the third Blood Reaper rushing with a club in one hand and a sword in the other. He did not wish to fight anymore, lest he grow too accustomed to it. Baelin wound up before launching the short sword for his assailant. The blade twirled in the hazy air before penetrating his heart with shocking accuracy. He fell onto his pierced chest and slid in the dirt.

With three of his archrivals dead about his feet, Baelin turned to face the masked "villager." The haughty reaper slowly unsheathed the dueling blades from his back and menacingly whirled them in his hands. This assassin knew all about the paladin he was about to face, particularly, because he faced him once before. When Baelin met him by the mansion's gates, the reaper nodded.

"Something to say?" Baelin asked, whilst noticing that the main doors to the mansion remained ajar.

The masked reaper then declared in a known voice, "Now, I can finish what I started with that meager scar on your neck."

There was no forgetting the origins of his scars, for Baelin used each one as a reminder of his journey. The one on his neck came from a duel with a vengeful assassin in Babylonia. His heart skipped a beat just at the thought of reuniting with him here like this. Even worse was the thought of him turning into a Blood Reaper. It was a tragic end for a man given the second chance.

Baelin scowled and said, "I trust that your wounds have healed well?"

Taking off the mask that hid his recognizable face, the reaper replied with resentment, "On the outside."

Seeing that his fears had come to fruition, he asked of him, "Why? How could you submit yourself to this wretched cause? A man like you does not surrender to dishonor. Instead of combating the reapers that sucked your father into their scheming hands, you, yourself, have joined them! Did you learn nothing of our duel over a year ago?"

"As I remember, the duel was to the death, and yet, here we both stand. You should fear me this time, paladin." He said.

Having accepted his wicked turn, Baelin answered, "I fear no man. You are a Blood Reaper and, so, I shall deal with you as I have dealt with most reapers of the same sort. Before I end your life, you will tell me what you have done to the woman inside that house. Let me know the truth, or I will finish you badly."

"She is with Kirik Cainam as we speak." The man snickered and then casually advanced into the battleground.

"With what?" Baelin wasted no time in meeting his rival for the final confrontation, for her life surely held in the balance.

They met steel before the mansion and fought with great fury. Indeed, the assassin's skill had blossomed since their last meeting. With all of his hatred, his blades stung true against the paladin's mace. His rage was projected painstakingly into each strike – each maneuver. Baelin knew that there was only one way to slacken his adversary's imperious onslaught.

He calculated each attack until a clear opening from below revealed itself, for Baelin's mace could shatter mistakes. The reaper kicked him to the ground, but the paladin rolled on his back and rose to his feet again. When the battle became so heated that it was hard to tell who would come out the victor, Baelin dodged a deadly swipe of the blade and bashed in the reaper's knee. He dropped to the ground, and lost one of his blades in the fall. Baelin was sure to retrieve it.

As the maimed assassin struggled to rise with his good leg, Baelin lay the mace down and held the blade firmly, saying, "If you were still a man of honor, I would have finished you well. But you chose a path of disgrace and so shall you meet its end."

The enraged reaper raised his sword and scrambled over to slay his most hated foe, drowning out the pain with abhorrence. When he was close enough, Baelin spun about to elude the sword and came around to cut off his head. The blade hacked straight through the reaper's neck and his body fell limp onto the ground. The head followed like a melon and rolled to his twitching feet.

Disgusted with what had just happened, Baelin tossed the bloody blade away as if it was cursed and reclaimed the Divine Mace. He raced back into the haunted mansion with a thirst for answers. Searching everywhere, he finally screamed her name in the hopes of a return. There was nothing. Only the echoes of spirits entered his ears.

Then, from the fathoms of the mansion's innards, a call came to him, "Paladin! Come join us!"

The voice was indistinct, like two voices put together. It sounded from upstairs. Thus, he ran up to the second floor and put the light of his mace before his path. It was the sound of a sorcerer, or a demon. Whatever it was, it resounded again, "Paladin! Return to us!"

Closer now, Baelin cried back, "Where are you?"

When there was no answer, he made it to the balcony overlooking the first floor of the elaborate cocktail lounge. As he looked down upon the hall, he heard the muffled cry of a female close by. Looking to the left side, he noticed that the library door was ajar and emitting a strange blue light. He did not notice it before, but there was no doubt that the sinister calling had come from inside there.

Carefully, he inched up to the door and held the mace tightly to his breast. Hearing her moans clearly now, Baelin stole a look into the library. To his great dismay, a scene seized his heart and mind. Like a dazed child, he stepped into the frame of the door and considered what kind of hell had taken him now.

Inside the atrium of the library, a most powerful warlock held Gideon up by her throat with one hand and smiled like the devil himself. Cloaked in a derelict black mantle, his chest bore the partially veiled breastplate of the old order of paladins. It was blackened by soot or ash, as were his plated cuisse and greaves. Yet, his features struck the fiercest blow. Pumping veins of blue afflicted his face like a cancer and his eyes were almost wholly black like a shark.

"Welcome back, Arl Baelin." The wicked sorcerer hissed, "My countenance has changed since you last saw me."

Mocking her with every word, he laughed under his breath. Baelin could hardly understand the disturbing scene. In his angst, he groaned, "Who the hell are you?"

"Do you not remember my face?" The sorcerer morphed his ominous face into that of Cletus Crow, the herald of Chimera.

In shock, Baelin gasped, "Cletus?"

Laughing as his faced returned to its horrid state, he said, "No. A stage name. You may call me Kirik Cainam. That is my true name — the name of the Blood Reapers."

Watching him hold Gideon without mercy, Baelin cried out, "You are the new leader, then?"

"New leader?" Cainam sneered, "I have been the leader since the beginning. I alone have fed off their souls. I alone have tasted their victories in the darkness. You only killed a pawn, Arl Baelin! Your vengeance was but a jest — a farce to amuse me!"

In seconds, his world began to unravel. All this time, he was certain that he had sacrificed his righteousness for the leader's life. Yet, it was far from the truth. This meant that Gideon, as well, was bested by Cainam's deception. Now, all of the fibers within Baelin's soul wished for this heinous man's demise.

"You had best release her." He said through his teeth, wounded by the sorcerer's venomous words.

Cainam scornfully caressed Gideon's beaten face and then dropped her at his feet. She held her throat and feebly gasped for air. Admiring his work on her, Cainam continued, "We have met twenty years ago on this very day. You were just a child then and scared out of your little wits, but that night changed both of our lives forever. I could have slit your woman's throat here and now, as I did with your sister, and sanctify your future once more."

It was all clear to him that his past had ultimately come back to haunt him. Mason never told him what happened to the fallen paladin that tried to kill his family that fateful night. His maddening eyes had awakened Baelin from many sleeps since childhood. Mason would not have knowingly put him in harm's way. Kirik Cainam had deceived even the New Vatican.

"Then again, I should kill you first, so that this spiteful bitch can bleed out without her man coming to the rescue." Cainam proceeded, "That night, I fell from grace and lifted you up into the eyes of the Paladin's Sanctum. My suffering fed your glory. Since then, I have so wished to reverse that cycle. Tonight, that shall pass. You have fallen from grace, Arl Baelin, and when you were just about to rise up to take a breath, I shall snag you under for good. This time, your fall shall give way to my rise.

"So, paladin, you will not fall without the opportunity to choose. I give you this ultimatum. Before I kill you, one other party will meet the same end. Will it be your woman here or the innocent village just down the street? One will die, but the choice I give to you. Make your final decree, oh great knight, or I kill them all."

It seemed like living a nightmare. His early teachers of the bible said that God returns your enemies. This great test had Baelin shaking in offence of that proverb. Was he to sacrifice the woman that loved him no more for the village that beseeched him for help? Was he bold enough to forsake the village that could potentially attest to his heroism in order to salvage his wife as a final petition for love and forgiveness?

His anger shook greater in thinking of the nerve that his enemy had to offer him an ultimatum. That was when it struck. There was but one paladin here. He did not listen to ultimatums from the likes of evil. Baelin would offer Cainam a challenge of his own. Manic, he gripped the Divine Mace with rage and screamed as he charged at his foe.

As Baelin came in to thrash him into a bloody pulp, Cainam quickly raised his hand and discharged a great surge of magic. The casting was as cobalt lightening that rattled the paladin's bones while sending him soaring backwards into the air. The charge took him over the hall below and into the opposite balcony where he finally smashed through the frail railing, through the door, and into the music room. There he tumbled into the brittle piano, causing it to break apart.

While true paladins were practically invulnerable to such magic, they were quite susceptible to crashing into things. Coughing, Baelin pushed himself off the rubble stricken floor and shook off the pain. For any other man would have been overcooked, he dared to rise to his knee and ignore the rattling effects of his counterpart's sorcery.

In the blow, he misplaced the mace. There was no time for lamentations, however, for Cainam had leapt over the entire hall and plunged into the music room in a single bound. The sorcerer recovered and rose to his feet without trouble, laying his sights on the fallen paladin. Baelin, on the other hand, was not the type to kneel to any adversary.

He spit out lingering blood onto the floor before saying jadedly, "Is that all?"

Cainam smiled and charged a greater magic in his fists. The ensuing fight was one-sided at best, since Baelin was still weak from the curse and the incantation. Cainam repelled any strike and delivered fierce counters, sending the paladin into furniture and debris. Onto his knees again, Baelin struggled to catch his breath. The sorcerer walked over to the gaping hole in the doorway and peered over the hall, confident that he had time.

Seeing that Gideon was gone, Cainam sighed, "Rodents run, but always deeper into the maze."

"You should know." Baelin said from behind him.

As Cainam turned to meet his prey, Baelin surprised him with an unyielding punch to the jaw. Surprised by the hit, the sorcerer fell back and plummeted down into the cocktail lounge. He collapsed a table in his drop. From the second floor, Baelin was able to locate the Divine Mace in the midst of the hall below.

He would need to join his archrival in the lounge in order to retrieve it.

Bleeding from his thrashing moments ago, Baelin took a deep breath and ran for the stairs. The only way to defeat Cainam was through sheer overpowering of the mace. While racing for the steps, he heard the sorcerer's voice, "You're weak. The hex has taken its toll on you, has it not? It made you fragile and delivered the elusive witch into my hands, for which there is no escape."

After making it down the steps, Baelin crept into the hall to look out for his enemy. Instead, he found his mace in the hands of the enemy. Taken aback, he took cover behind a worn sofa and clenched his fist in anger. Kirik Cainam neared closer to his position, snickering as he ambled, "How ironic would it be if I bludgeoned the paladin with his own mace?"

The sorcerer was wise and calculating, but his vindictive pride was what Baelin focused on the most. He slithered from one hiding place over to another, and so on, until Cainam faced the other direction. That was when he struck from the dark. Despite his wounds, Baelin pounced upon him with great skill. But, it was not enough. Cainam clenched him by the throat.

"Springing upon me like a cat will not do you well, Arl Baelin. I can detect you in this place." Cainam flung him into the bar table and came over to finish him there.

When Cainam came down with the mace, Baelin mustered his stamina and narrowly avoided the devastating assault. The mace blasted through the bar table with ease, sending shards of wood and marble everywhere. In the middle of the wreckage, Baelin immediately countered by catching Cainam's arm off-guard and snapping his wrist.

After the sorcerer let the mace drop in sudden agony, Baelin followed with a fast punch to the face. When his enemy winced back, he salvaged the Divine Mace and said in-between pants, "Idiot, you should stick to sorcery."

Losing patience, Kirik Cainam simply replied, "Yes."

He charged up another spell and forcefully pressed his open hand onto the carpeted floor. A great quake shook the hall as a drop in a pool of water. The shockwave tore up the floorboards and demolished everything in its path. Baelin dove to the floor and covered his head as the debris rained down like the apocalypse. The cocktail lounge transformed into a warzone.

After the disaster was over, Baelin rose from the rubble. Cainam was there to greet him with a backhand that sent him into further ruins of the mansion, resuming the fight. Lying on his belly, he witnessed the sorcerer channel some sort of dark energy. As the sinister force entered his evil void, his wrist had fully healed. In dread, Baelin pushed himself off the floor and rushed to slay him before he healed further grievances.

When Baelin swung the mace for his head, Cainam caught it in the palm of his hand and struck him across the face in riposte. Blood spurted from his mouth as he stumbled back from the strike. His temporary daze let Cainam's final maneuver breathe. The sorcerer grasped him by the throat again and began to drain the life force from his very being.

Baelin could feel his life transfer into his enemy's hand, burning his arteries and cramping his muscles. Staring into Cainam's black eyes struck fear in his heart. And still, his wrath made him feel entitled to triumph. His penance was not yet complete. His duties were far too great.

In defiance, Baelin brought down the might of his mace and fractured his enemy's skull. Cainam jolted backwards and released his prize, holding his head instead. The minute the sorcerer answered with a bolt of lightning from his outstretched hand, Baelin twirled away from its course and brought the mace around with both hands. The telling blow sprayed fragments of bone and blood into the air.

Kirik Cainam fell to the warped floor and moved no more. Battered, the true paladin glared down upon his fallen enemy and sighed in grief. He staggered away from the sorcerer's remains and pondered over the terrible events of the afternoon. The house-cleansing mission had spiraled out of control. Before he could finish what he came for in the first place, Baelin had to find Gideon and ensure her safety.

However, from behind him, groaning and the subtle movement of rubble sounded. The noises were not welcoming. As sure as Baelin could see with his own two eyes, the sorcerer stretched out his arms and sucked in the dark energy of the mansion yet again. He could feel the spirits' auras rushing into Cainam's body like a vacuum.

In the meantime, his mangled bloody head gradually started to heal once more. Gazing on in horror, Baelin finally understood that he exploited the mansion's sinister energy for his own soul. As he would drain the life from others, so was he feeding off Midvein Mansion. As long as they fought in this place, Cainam would never truly be defeated.

So Baelin ran passed his enemy and raced for the stairway, pushing rubble out of his way as he scurried forth. He had to lure him out of the house. Hurdling over smashed furnishings and statues, the paladin pressed out of the demolished hall and pushed for the highest level of the mansion. His case and other personal objects awaited his return in the master bedroom. He had to make it there as fast as possible.

Upon reaching the door that read, "You will burn," Baelin hastily shoved his way in. Now that the demon had reclaimed the house, Cainam could revel in its power without hindrance. He hid within the shrouded corner of the room and waited. All the while, the drainage of energy stopped. The sorcerer was making his way to find him. Baelin prayed that he did not find Gideon first, if she was still here.

Cainam shouted as he advanced up the stairway, knowing that Baelin could hear him, "I thrived in this house for years, licking my wounds and partaking in its nourishing properties! You had slept here yourself, but I bet you never considered the library! You could not imagine the knowledge I received from reading the books of our ancestors!

"This is wisdom from the age before our own! Before the Primeval Tragedy, this library has served as our own little Garden of Eden! It holds the secrets of our past, our greatest victories and worst failures! Now I possess the erudition of a thousand ages! Even Ellium hasn't come close to what I have researched!"

He was close now and, because he could sense Baelin's probable whereabouts, Cainam shattered the doors in the hallway to uncover his exact location. Reaching the master bedroom, the sorcerer scorched the door into a fiery blanket of ashes and entered. He sensed his prey close by.

Yet, something caught his attention first. In the far left corner of the room, the paladin's case rested under a rite of protection. Cainam grinned and approached it, remembering his own holy case when he was of the paladin order. That little opening was all that Baelin needed to rush his archrival.

From the shadows, he cried and tackled Cainam with mace in hand, blasting him through the oval window. Amongst the shattered glass, they fell down to the next story and landed harshly onto the grand verandah's roof. Rolling in temporary pain, the two rivals recovered and continued their fight outside under the falling sun.

Baelin challenged Cainam with a ferocity not yet seen. He beat him with heavy swings of the mace and staunch strikes from every limb. The sorcerer was no stranger to such fiery bouts. He, in turn, met the paladin head on with greater blows and spells. Nonetheless, as Baelin had expected, Cainam's new lacerations were not healing. The fight had evened out and he was not going to stop until the sorcerer was routed.

Despite Baelin's promising performance in single combat, Kirik Cainam deflected a weak assault and made him pay for it. With a powerful elbow to the lower back, Baelin flopped to the roof in a sudden throbbing. Cainam then delivered a fierce kick to the stomach that brought him over to the verandah's edge. Below, the crows cawed to his doom.

The trodden sorcerer sauntered over to his aching adversary and stepped on the Divine Mace, then crouching down to snap Baelin's neck. The paladin tried to resist with all his might, but the sorcerer had a greater strength than anticipated. Just when all seemed hopeless, a cry came from the verandah's screen doors, "Cainam!"

There Gideon stood, waving her arms and chanting a spell. Cainam dropped his archrival's neck, though not removing foot from mace, and laughed, "How delightful! The whore returns to put on a show! Have you not learned that your magic has no effect on me? I retain my paladin attributes! It is a matter of science, not righteousness!"

Still, Gideon did not falter. In concluding her casting, she spread out her arms and produced a purple flash than vanished as soon as it came. And as Cainam was about to joke, the sounds of cawing and flapping wings resonated from below. The crows swarmed the sorcerer relentlessly, compelling him to flail his arms and remove his boot from Baelin's mace.

It was a great distraction, for Baelin lifted his mace and batted Cainam's right knee. Hearing it crunch, he rose up onto his own knee and flailed a vertical strike into the rogue's jaw. The wallop was unwavering as it brought blood from his mouth. Kirik Cainam tumbled off the verandah and plummeted stories down onto the rickety fence out front. The fallen paladin should have known that God was the greatest scientist.

When it was over, the crows flew away, leaving Baelin and Gideon on the verandah alone. She crouched down and let her heart rate lessen, for she was fraught and hurt. After taking the time he needed, Baelin peered down at his greatest enemy. He lay motionless on the ground, his voice silenced.

Gideon had come back to rescue him, and for that, he needed to tend to her. Baelin ran over and took her in his arms, caressing her bruised face. Not since three years back, did she do the same for him. Yet, on this day, Gideon touched his cheek and had the humility to utter, "You are hurt."

"But alive," He said while beaming down on her, "We are both alive."

After the hell they had experienced in such a short time, their hearts grew lighter for each other. It took the will to fight as common allies to ignite the fire that remained imprisoned for so long. They sat in the quiet of the early evening and basked in each other's presence. While the final task of cleansing the house of spirits was yet at hand, Baelin needed to care for his wife first. The night was still young.

Redeem the Knight
Altruism VIII

Six months ago…

Back home in Linden, his dearest friend, Ronald Tumbler, implored Arl Baelin for his holy services. Just returning from prayer, Arl naturally agreed to help him. Arl followed Ronald back to his house with concern for who was ill. Upon entering through the backdoor, they converged in his bedroom to heal his best friend's best friend.

To Arl's surprise, Ronald's German Shepard lay sick on his bed with no signs of improvement. His wife was cursing at him, blaming the dog for ruining their bed sheets. Nevertheless, it was clear that Ronald loved his dog, as it was loyal and protective of his children. Though fuddled at first, Arl embraced his friend and took serious of his request.

"There are really sick people outside of this house and you force Islandia's paladin to cure your damn dog?" His wife said.

"He's more than a dog, Margaret, he's family! So get used to it, woman!" Ronald retorted.

The poor canine looked into Arl's eyes with fear, unknowing of his abilities. Without any further delay, Arl placed his hand over the dog's sweaty fur and lowered his head in prayer. It was perplexing for many who studied the paladins' so called "blessed hand" skill. Only true paladins possessed this gift.

Some argued that it was God's gift to a select group so that they might serve the masses as Jesus did in the archaic age. Others blamed it on the post-apocalyptic blend of enigmatic elements and unforeseen human design. Was it a miracle or was it magical? Regardless of its origins, paladins, like the sorcerers of the era, were dying out with each passing generation. It was a strong argument for nonbelievers.

But for Arl and those who received his blessings, the blessed hand was testament to God's reclamation of the world. In moments, the dog began to move about the bed. Once Arl let loose of him, he leapt off the bed altogether and wagged his tail. There was an immediate awareness for Ronald's pet, for he understood that the paladin rid the disease from his system.

The Tumbler house was exuberant in their gratitude for saving their friend, even Margaret. After treating Arl to supper in the kitchen, Ronald could not help noticing that his dog was entranced with the paladin that helped him. In fact, he licked Arl's hand and barked happily around his seat. At that moment, there was no question in how Ronald was going to repay his lifelong comrade.

At the table, Ronald swallowed his bread and said, "Arl, how are you faring out there these days?"

Grinning, he replied, "Surviving."

"Surviving alone." Ronald interjected.

When it was clear that Arl had no direct response, Ronald proceeded, "I want you to take my dog with you."

Bemused by his ally's shocking offer, Arl stammered, "Ron, I couldn't—"

"He has chosen you, man. You see?" Ronald pointed to the canine's fixation on him, "I found him in the streets. He is a survivor like you. You came here for a reason, Arl, and I think this is it right here."

Looking at the faithful hound, Arl said, "How do I know that he wants to go with me?"

As the dog licked his face, Ronald snickered, "He just let you know, adventure boy. Besides, Margaret will be the next one you'll have to heal if he stays here any longer. Isn't that right, my little octopus?"

Amidst Margaret shaking her head, Arl decided to accept his friend's generous gift and stroked the hound's head. While it hurt him to see his loyal hound go, Ronald recognized that Arl was in desperate need of a companion. Be it man or beast, a companion is honey that sweetens with time. It can save the lonely at heart.

His new companion was sure to join him in his adventures out in the great unknown. The dog bounced as he followed Arl out the door under the cover of night. Ronald asked what he was going to name him now that the dog belonged to him. Petting the dog's chin, it became obvious. That night, Arl and his dog, Alec, went off to start their new life as one. They would come to share their grief and their joy as partners in survival.

Now in Midvein Mansion, six months later...

In the company of the sinking sun, Baelin placed Gideon's weary frame onto the master bed. His bedroll covered the grime and ash. The intense battle between archrivals left the mansion in feeble condition, even more so than it was already. From the shattered oval window, fading rays of the sun lit up the bedroom and accentuated the floating dust particles within.

After brief moments of silence between them, Gideon broke it in saying, "This is what I get for helping you."

Baelin nodded in support of her statement, but then had the mettle to ask, "Why did you tell everyone that I killed you?"

"It was a ploy." She replied immediately, almost expecting the question, "With the witch dead, reapers and covetous buffoons would surely test our homeland. You should see the vermin we baited in."

"You should have seen what that did to my name." Baelin said, unmoved by her reasoning.

Gideon looked into his revealing eyes and laid her head back down, lamenting, "Our love was cursed from the beginning."

While he wanted to say otherwise, it was difficult to prove her mistaken. For now, Baelin just admired her beautiful face and attractive figure, riddled with welts and abrasions. He thought of his wife being stripped of her honor three years back, and it stifled his heart. At least he could protect her now.

"I must heal you." He said, "Your wounds are angry."

"Leave me. Tend to your house." She rolled over to her side, facing the dying sun.

Time was running out and he had to focus on completing his mission—the mission bequeathed by the Paladin's Sanctum and approved by means of the New Vatican. As paladin, Baelin aroused his duties and left his wife there to rest. Ready for round two, he took his case downstairs and into the basement for the rite of cleansing. By the uncanny sounds echoing throughout the halls, the mansion's evil spirit was less than pleased.

Standing in cold, sickening water, Baelin removed the contents of his case yet again. He prayed for protection from the demon that would no doubt try to interrupt the ritual. This time, he held onto the mace and let it shine brightly while starting the rite, causing the basement to resonate and howl.

Nonetheless, he followed through with it, reading from the Holy Bible first and then the Compendium, forcefully proclaiming the words. The demon was defiant, screaming and cursing in an ancient language. Baelin had performed such rites before, but this sinister spirit was powerful. It had held onto the mansion for hundreds of years and was not going to let go of it without a fight.

While proceeding with the ritual, the infuriated demon sounded as if it was coming down the stairs to find him. He could have been frightened, but he trusted in the power of Christ to defend him. The Compendium and bible refer to Jesus as the champion of exorcists, driving out demons wherever they lingered. The paladins were true to this method and evoked Jesus's name during all cleansing rites.

The demon made it inside the basement, spattering the water across the way violently as it neared closer. Having memorized the rest of the rite, Baelin tossed the Compendium back into the case and held the mace forward with both hands. He shouted the last words vehemently as the evil spirit raced in for the possession. Upon finishing his last prayer, Baelin cried out and slammed the glowing mace into the water with great might.

The water splashed all about the darkness of the dungeon, submerging the mace's light. When he pulled his weapon out from the water, the basement illuminated as before, but with silence. Droplets progressively fell back to whence it came, soaking the paladin further. At the end of his taxing mission to Midvein Mansion, an ancient demon was driven out and a living one was propelled off the roof.

Moments later…

Baelin took what little rations he had left in his case and shared them with Gideon upstairs to watch the sunset. The plan was to sleep the night away in an old mansion and revisit Chimera in the morning, but Kirik Cainam's unfavorable visit changed all that. He planned to deliver Cainam's head to the village as a peace offering and a forewarning. Did they know that their "missing" villagers had become Blood Reapers, or were they reapers all along?

Pondering this, he walked out onto the verandah and peered down at the bodies he left scattered out front. There were only four. To his dismay, Kirik Cainam was gone. Blood lay as the only proof of him even being there. Suddenly, the house did not feel so safe. There were no tracks that led him to believe that his corpse was taken. The only person who would have moved his body was himself.

Restless, Baelin dashed back into the house and removed Gideon's crude dagger from his case. He placed it into her baffled hands, saying, "If anyone enters this room, scream."

The time to dawdle was over. Without her consent, Baelin placed his hands on her and tried to heal her injuries. Gideon fought him back, groaning, "What do you think you're doing, paladin?"

"I am healing you, whether you like it or not!" He replied.

Fighting him all the way, she shouted, "Get your hands off of me, damn it!"

Finally, Baelin grabbed her wrists and cried, "Cainam's body isn't there!"

There they remained silent and motionless, shocked by the impossible truth. In the end, they shared a common enemy more terrifying than they could have known. Feeling vulnerable, Gideon gave in to the paladin and allowed him to heal her serious injuries. She had always feared his curative techniques would smother her magical core. Yet, if it meant her life, she succumbed.

She lay fidgety on the bedroll as Baelin worked his way up her legs, than to her torso, and finally her appendages. Healing only the worst abrasions, he made it up to her face and looked into her eyes, taken by flash visions of her from years back. Gideon, sensing that he was staring at her, turned her head to meet his gaze. The moment was awkward enough for him to pull away before his heart ached.

"I have to go." He said, wiping her blood from his hands.

Gideon lifted her head and asked, "Where are you going?"

Baelin replied as he headed for the door, "To search the house for him."

"He's gone." She said in return, "I do not sense him any longer. You are wasting your time."

Baelin trusted in her foresight. Stopping at the doorway, he thought about the circumstances of Cainam's awakening. If he was alive, one place beckoned him. When in the library, he offered the paladin an ultimatum. Baelin shook at the thought of Cainam keeping his word. He pledged to kill them all.

He turned his head out towards the window and exclaimed, "Chimera. He is going to the village!"

"To hell with them!" She griped, "You can hardly fight, let alone – "

Baelin gripped the mace with a sudden thirst for retribution and interposed, "Find a place to hide. I vow to return after I have wrenched out his beating heart and bashed his skull to dust."

Gideon stood at the open window to watch Baelin equip a scabbard onto his belt. He sheathed one of the reapers' blades and collected some throwing knives from their straps. Heading for the village on foot, the paladin secured the satchel to his back and let the Divine Mace sleep until the time came. The sun had vanished beneath the horizon, concealing him from sight. As one mission concluded, a newer one had beckoned the call.

At last, Baelin recovered from a slight limp and marched towards the village with full steps. His healing abilities as paladin were faster than any ordinary man's reconstructive qualities. This blessing also strengthened his immune system, giving him an edge against most opponents. He would need these biological aptitudes if he had to face Kirik Cainam a second time.

Because of his rage, the trip to Chimera did not take as long as routine. Baelin saw the torches of the north gate and performed an equipment check one last time as he proceeded. As expected, Cletus Crow was not standing guard. It was night anyway, and not many were likely to be up and about. Yet, upon entering the vacant gate, Baelin found the village to be calmer than he had predicted.

It seemed derelict. Passing the security post and stable on his right and hospital on his left, there was no one to be seen. The cadence of his footsteps in the gravel was the only sound amongst the unnerving stillness. The paladin then passed the church on his far left and the vacant meeting hall on his right side. It was not late enough for the village to behave as a ghost town.

By the Chief's Manor, on the other hand, two recognizable guards stood watch outside the main door. They saw him approaching from a distance and turned to look at each other as he advanced. Baelin walked up to them and wriggled his pendent fingers, expecting anything. They said nothing to him. Instead, they both gave permission to proceed inside. Sensing the peculiarities, he stepped inside with full guard.

The double doors leading into the hall were open this time around and Baelin easily spotted Chief Hared standing on his usual platform in his arrogant stance. He walked inside, surveying his surrounding all the way. When the paladin reached the middle of the room, Hared folded his arms and said, "Paladin, your presence is welcomed. Judging by your contusions, I would say that the house is putting up quite a fight."

"The house is cleansed." Baelin said, unmoved by the chief's sardonic tone.

"Well, that is splendid news indeed!" He replied merrily.

"Indeed." Baelin cynically rejoined, "I also found your 'missing' villagers."

Changing his demeanor, Hared declared contemptuously, "Have you now? Well, where are they?"

"I killed them." Baelin said nonchalantly, rolling over Hared's muddled start, "They were Blood Reapers. In their try to ambush me, I dispatched them—all four of them."

After a stroppy silence, Hared only uttered, "I see."

"I am glad that you see, being that you are the chief of all these villagers." Baelin continued boldly, "This leaves me to wonder. There can only be two possible solutions. One: they were turned into reapers, in which the leader pours his tainted blood down their throats and, subsequently, turns them into his little lackeys, or two: they were Blood Reapers all along.

"Either one of those should scare you, since you are responsible for the people who live here. Where are all of your villagers, Hared? They usually greet me with odious gazes. And what of Cletus Crow? I am almost certain that he is lurking about somewhere. Perchance he is being treated at your hospital?"

Chief Hared returned his hands behind him and, while walking over to the podium nearby, professed, "There was a small little community of drifters who lived here when we arrived. They would drift from one place to another until Kirik Cainam moved in."

Baelin, discerning his enemy's identity, listened to Hared's disturbing affirmation further, "He gave us all a haven—a place to call home. We fed off those vermin for months, though it was not nearly enough to sustain us. Therefore, we behaved as drifters ourselves, attracting merchants and wanderers alike. At last, the greatest moth has befallen upon our flame."

As eight armed reapers emerged from the darkness to surround the paladin, Hared crooned from behind the podium, "We shall make our master proud this night, for the lion has met his end in the snake's den!"

The reapers surrounded him from all angles, some laughing and some growling. The most decorated one met the chief at the podium and removed the whip from his belt, grinning at the paladin with memorable features. Within seconds, Baelin pegged him as being the nervy villager who swept the church floor while he went in to pray. The entire village was occupied.

As his minions encircled Baelin, Chief Hared looked to his secondary and said loud enough for the paladin to hear, "Try to kill him with his own mace. Cainam would like that."

Baelin clenched the Divine Mace in his right hand and lingered his left over the sheathed blade, pleading all of heaven to bless him with the might to survive the oncoming trial. Out of the seven reapers that cordoned him, one of the younger ones charged up from behind to spark the onslaught. Hence, Baelin unsheathed the blade in his left hand and fought for his very life.

His great skill in battle warded off some of the more cautious slayers. Nonetheless, the brave reapers that did rush in for the attack were enough. Baelin, fortunately, knocked one off his feet and delivered a final blow with the mace. The strike crushed his skull into the floorboards, removing one goon from the fight. Dispatching the first reaper did not come without a price, however. A she-demon leapt onto his back and sunk her yellow teeth into his neck.

While he was able to fling her off, Baelin suffered a crude gash in his flesh. He spun about to crack her in the shoulder with the mace before reforming a defensive stance. The proceeding combat was gruesome, for these reapers were relentless. He could think of nothing else but slaying his foes before they did him in first. Of all the cursing and sweating, Baelin outmaneuvered an opponent and slit his throat with the subtle slice of the blade.

The second reaper collapsed to the ground and bled to death. Baelin, meeting the rest in bloody contest, despised such carnage. He had seen enough of it in his nightmares and did not wish to find redemption by way of the sword. The sudden cut over his face awakened him from any worry. Blood leaked down his face and bore a smarting pain. He could not falter again.

Incensed, Baelin rushed under a swinging ax, slashed a reaper's waist, and then stabbed him in the back of the neck with the same tainted blade. Another advanced to cut him in two, but he was able to block the strike with his mace and remove the blade form the third quarry's neckline. As the reaper fell to the ground, coloring the floorboards red, Baelin deflected the second strike from his insistent enemy and proceeded to exchange blows.

While fighting, he noticed that Chief Hared had disappeared from the podium, leaving only the decorated secondary there wielding the whip. A coward's scheme. Baelin, in the meantime, accumulated welts and lesions from the fierce contest. Kirik Cainam had bled him enough already. Again, a brief break in his concentration merited a spear to his lower back.

He cried out from the sudden aching sting and pulled away from the point's reach, content on taking him out when the chance came. But then, a reaper struck the blade from his left hand, leaving him with the Divine Mace as his only weapon. Baelin had no patience for pain. In a well-timed counterattack, he broke his attacker's kneecap with one swing of the mace and then came back to fracture his forehead with the pommel.

The kneeling reaper fell backwards and bled out onto the floor. Soon after, the remaining warriors fought over a slippery coating of commingled blood. An overeager foe ultimately slid and fell to her knee, presenting Baelin with the opportunity for a critical strike. Dodging the ax a second time, he capitalized on the reaper's fall and broke her jaw with a savage rising blow.

The Divine Mace was no match for her resolve. She, too, met her end in the puddle of reaper blood. Again, the spearman sprinted in for another chance to impale the paladin. This time, Baelin evaded the thrust, broke off the head, and spun about to return the broken edge into the wielder's eye socket. The maneuver was swift as it was ferocious, for the sixth reaper was defeated. At last, the whip wielding fiend on the platform seemed to be losing his smirk.

Briefly eyeing his decorated adversary could have killed him, for the axman came in for a powerful kill strike. Baelin turned about and used the mace as a shield to parry the blow. Though he avoided a grisly death, he lost his mace and tumbled to the ground. When trying to rise in order to meet his enemy in combat once again, the reaper from behind seized him by the throat with the infamous whip. The decorated Blood Reaper finally served a fatal purpose. Unarmed and detained, Baelin calculated how he would survive the next swing of the ax.

Years ago when he was but a teen, Legion Leader Mason taught him the hell of war. He learned that war was built in the hearts of all men since childhood and it would emerge regardless of how hard one tried to suppress it. After various trainings in combat, it was clear than when all hope was lost in the heat of the fight, only survival mattered. Through survival, the victim could become the victor if they accepted the instinctual spirit of war that lay dormant within. Only when cornered does the rat become most dangerous.

Ensnared by the whip, Baelin rolled to his side and let the axman drop the blade into the floor. He mechanically noticed the reaper's sheathed dagger attached to the belt and removed it during his evasion. Stabbing his enemy in the back of the knee, Baelin grasped the taut thong of the whip and cast the newly bloodied dagger for the secondary's face. The instantaneous attack caught the decorated reaper off guard, for the knife mined deep into his throat and brought him to his back.

The unyielding axman tried for another vertical hack, but by mistake, sliced through the whip itself. As Baelin designed it, he rolled free from the reaper's sight and snapped his neck from the side. His eyes widened and his body fell limp. In the company of the clunking of the ax to the floor were the last gurgles of the fading secondary. By his own amazement, Baelin had slain all eight Blood Reapers.

As he half-heartedly admired his work, the paladin took deep breaths and started to feel the consequences of winning. The new gashes and bruises about his body were disconcerting. A taste of blood from the running lesion on his cheek wet his dry tongue. Then, the smarting of the bite in his neck gave him grief. These were quintessential Blood Reapers and, like cockroaches, eight of them meant that there were masses more hidden about.

Moments later...

The two guards outside of the manor noticed the lasting minutes of silence and decided to venture inside to help with the cleaning efforts. What they found was a scene of slaughter. All eight of their kin were slain, but the paladin was nowhere in sight. It did not seem possible that one man could have defeated all of the warriors at once and yet live.

Further investigation of the failed ensnarement led the guards to Hared's secondary, stabbed in the throat and keyless. Then their hearts dropped. The paladin did not escape, but rather infiltrated their underground lair by means of the hidden door below the podium. It was still unclear as to how long he had been inside the tunnels, but they feared the worst. They just imagined what a man who was capable of killing eight men at once could do when rewarded with the element of surprise.

Chief Hared, however, waited inside the underground control office free from care. His three assistants planned the feast of the paladin for the evening's celebrations when a knock came about the door. Only one of them thought it strange that Hared's secondary knocked. He never knocked.

When the oblivious chief went to make certain that it was his deputy, Baelin kicked the door in, rapping Hared in the head. The grand entrance caught them all by surprise, for his throwing knives did not miss their marks. He hastily cast his small blades into the reapers' vulnerable parts, aiming for the eyes or throat. In a matter of seconds, Hared became the only living one left.

Baelin seized him by the neck and slammed him against the wall, peering into his trembling eyes. The overtaken chief could not believe what was happening, for the paladin was severely beaten, but very much alive. Having placed the Divine Mace back into the pouch strapped around his back, Baelin was not prepared to batter the sly scoundrel just yet. He wanted a query answered.

"Where is Cainam?" Baelin asked through his teeth, too drained to beat the answers out of him.

Ultimately realizing that he was outdone, Chief Hared eased his composure and started to laugh, saying crazily, "Kirik Cainam is watching, paladin. You should know! He is always watching!"

Amongst the demented cackling, Baelin effortlessly broke his neck with one hand. After the laughing stopped, he permitted Hared's lifeless body to hit the ground. The great ruse was over. The Blood Reapers' crafty hideout was exposed. Now that he entered the snake's den, Baelin needed to course through the tunnels and uncover its purpose. It vexed him to think about what they were hiding within the tunnels ahead.

Baelin considered Hared's corpse by his feet and shook his head in angst. Since the beginning of the mission, Chimera lured him in to their scheme. Even his path to redemption bled. Now, the only way out was in. The door to the tunnels beckoned him to open it and venture inside. He wondered if Cainam was waiting for him. He wondered if he could defeat him a second time, bruised and battered.

The administrative center, as it appeared, contained maps of Islandia with detailed directions. Documents of orders yet to be completed scattered all about the desks. Abductions and plots to wipe out Islandic officials were also among the papers. They were planning something major — something epic. Baelin stashed as many sensitive documents as he could fit into his satchel, crowding the mace that waited inside.

After a deep breath, he cautiously entered the tunnels and hid in the darkness. Baelin bypassed corridors that branched off into different directions and tried to follow the path that headed north. If the lair burrowed through the expanse of the village, then he could potentially find an exit route somewhere outside the surface walls. However, as he ventured deeper into the tunnels, Baelin gained a greater appreciation for the reapers' meticulous fabrication.

Coded signs directed them underneath the hospital, schoolhouse, meeting hall, and even the fake chapel. Under despairing circumstances, Baelin stealthily pounced upon unsuspecting dwellers and silenced them. One after the other, he snuffed reapers that wandered too close or stood in his way. In one desperate situation, there was no choice but to scuffle with a petty group. The element of surprise proved to be advantageous.

Leaving over a dozen corpses in his wake, Baelin came across the first significant intersection. The junction was large and mirrored one of the crossroads near the north gate. Clearly, he was on the right track, but there was no way to sneak through without being seen. There was a throng of reapers tussling and gambling, waiting for Hared's word that Baelin was either dead or captured. Torches dispersed about the area revealed the tents and miscellaneous goods that they stole from slain travelers.

He counted thirteen reapers. Baelin was inclined to charge into the valley of promising death when, from the left side of his concealment, a gift came ambling forth. An unaware Blood Reaper wielding a bow and quiver of arrows headed right for him. The offering was well received.

Starting with the isolated, Baelin began firing his arrows. One by one, he picked off unwary stragglers with fatal accuracy. It was not until one of the soaring arrows whistled in the fusty air that the reapers noticed they were under attack. To cause panic, the fleeing paladin placed an eager arrow into the back of one of the gamblers of the group. The cannibal cultists scurried about with anger and fear in their profanity.

Crates and mounds of drivel gave him cover for a while, for they estimated his location. When he thought that a clever reaper found him, Baelin rose into view and fired an arrow directly into his chest. The arrowhead pierced through to his back and sent him crashing down into the large basin of the junction. With only two arrows left, Baelin darted from behind the cover and sought to shoot from another spot. In the course of his run, a stout foe caught him in the jaw with a club.

The reaper hid in the darkness and brought Baelin to the ground, partly in a daze. The bow clunked out of reach and his challenger kicked the quiver away. As he tried to rise to his feet, the reaper struck him with a heavy knee and grabbed the shaft of his mace. Baelin took hold of the club and then delivered a devastating elbow to the knee that struck him. The reaper fell to his good knee and shouted. From there, the paladin shook off his own agony and battered the enemy with his own club.

Thereafter, Baelin heard the running of Blood Reapers coming in for the kill. He spit out a blood-soaked molar and awakened the Divine Mace from its sleep. Though beaten and exhausted, Islandia's paladin was not willing to surrender. He surrendered to God and that was enough. Until they gave in, Blood Reapers would be welcomed by the smiting of the mace.

Baelin watched them come for him, counting eight, and began to pray. "Our Father, who art in heaven, hallowed be thy name." A parry and then powerful blow to the face of one and then a sturdy kick to send him into the way of others. "Thy Kingdom come, thy will be done, on earth as it is in heaven." A punch in the jaw rattled one just enough for Baelin to clout another in the leg, tripping him, in advance of slewing them both.

"Give us this day our daily bread." After breaking one's collarbone, he absorbed a strong hit to the kidney. "And forgive us our trespasses," A vengeful forearm into the aggressor's neck provided an opening to counter another's oncoming attack, "as we forgive those who trespass against us." The battle raged on quickly and without hesitation, like teeming piranhas amidst a greater foe.

"And lead us not into temptation, but deliver us from evil." After defeating a crazed swordsman, Baelin leapt over the fallen reaper and walloped the other before he could retrieve a modified truncheon. When he buckled, the paladin kicked him over to ensure his demise. Amongst the internal sound of his heartbeat and resounding rhythm of his heavy panting, there was but one holy knight standing over the many corpses of the wicked. "For the kingdom, the power, and the glory are yours for ever and ever. Amen."

Baelin made his way into the center of the junction and ate of the bread that remained in the baskets. He guzzled water from cups and kneeled by the small fire. Above, small vents allowed the trivial smoke to rise out of the tunnels and dissipate. Just from looking up, his neck ached and his body throbbed. Using the extended mace as advantage for leaning, Baelin shut his eyes and permitted his body to recover for a while.

He appealed, "Lord, I am so tired. Give me the strength to overcome. I do not wish for blood, and yet blood covers my body and the path I walk. I am in your care, for you can do all things. Deliver me from this hell and guide my hands to serve as yours. If there is a purpose for me here, please let it be realized now."

Before any more Blood Reapers noticed his presence, Baelin rose to his feet and headed for the northern pass. He knew that he had to be close now, for the church and schoolhouse were behind him. There was no turning back. Any reapers in behind would surely alert the entire village of his slovenly escape. Time was of the essence.

Under the cover of darkness, Baelin bypassed loitering reapers and continued up the path. Eventually, he reached an even greater cavity. Within the cavern, Blood Reapers were busy at work. Red-cloaked cultists managed an altar with the reaper insignia in back. The design was always the same. It consisted of a smiling snake that coiled around a standing scythe. Further investigation of the scene revealed cryptic symbols that baffled the most esteemed symbologists.

Pews surrounded the eerie dais, able to seat at least one hundred followers. By the sacristy, a table beheld the elements needed to taint and drink blood. Plates, utensils, and naperies were all gathered neatly to the side. If there was a ceremony on the docket, it was happening very soon.

Panning towards the back of the cavern, Baelin noticed a long stretch of ligneous prison cells. The fate of the helpless detainees seized his heart, for he knew what awaited them. The cultists, no more than seven, were not warriors. Their purpose abided for the blood rituals in which those who were chosen to receive the blood of Kirik Cainam had to drink and become part of his sect. The wooden cells in back most likely caged the unwilling participants. Only God knew how many sufferers prayed for liberation from inside those compartments.

Then again, two crucial elements of the ceremony were still missing. The table on the altar served as the devouring slab. The sacrifice was to be placed on the slab, cut open, and served to the participants at the end of the ritual. Thus was the ceremonial rite of the Blood Reapers. Baelin scrutinized the cavern from the tunnel, but could not find Cainam among his minions. Nor could he guess the identity of the sacrifice. Fearing that reapers were on his trail, Baelin decided to act.

Crouched against the cavern's wall, Baelin hurried to a dark crook and avoided the torches. He waited there like a lion in the tall grass. Closer now, he inched towards the back of the altar and kept a vigilant eye on the hooded cultists. The occupied minions never noticed him there. When one ambled forth to tend to the element table, Baelin leaped out from his cover and crushed the reaper's head with a daring swing of the mace.

After the wasting of an unwary cultist, the six others turned about to witness Arl Baelin make his way onto their altar. He wielded the Divine Mace and kicked over the devouring table, presenting himself to his enemies. Though feeble, his appearance shocked them all to the core. One of them unsheathed a sacrificial dagger. When Baelin unsheathed his last throwing knife, the minion instinctively dropped the blade and raised his hands.

"Sit." Baelin groaned and started for them.

All six reluctantly sat in the pews, watching Islandia's paladin walk right passed them. With his mace, Baelin ruptured the lock on one of the ligneous compartments and cautiously opened the door. He looked back to check on the cultists before meeting the inhabitant of the indecent cell. Half-naked, the thin man rose to his feet and peered closely at his rescuer.

"Who are you?" The man asked, but quickly realized his savior's identity, "Are you Baelin? Are you the paladin?"

"I am." He replied solemnly, "Islandia has sent me to find you. What is your name?"

"Samuel. I am an Islandic soldier. There are more of us here —four more soldiers and over twenty civilians." He said.

Baelin surveyed the reapers again and said, "What is this?"

As the soldier stretched outside of his cell, he started, "They were saving us for the ceremonial feast. Tonight, we were the lucky candidates to be turned into Blood Reapers. Their leader is here and so is the sacrifice."

"Who is the sacrifice?" Baelin watched the hooded cultists with daggers in his eyes.

Samuel the soldier rejoined, "You."

With that, Baelin began hammering all of the locks off the cell doors. Samuel claimed that there was a weapon shed in the far corner of the cavern, so he went off to gather as much as he could muster. The cowards in their pews refused to try the paladin now that he released the missing soldiers. The soldiers, in turn, released the feeble civilians from their cruel keep.

A transcendent experience greeted Baelin after breaking open another door. Inside the cell, a young malnourished boy stood alone. He looked up at the paladin as if he was an angel. Baelin looked down upon him as if he was his own son, Alec. It was three long years without his boy. For six months, his canine companion filled the void of his son's tender presence, but this child seemed to reflect Alec's every feature. He would have been four years of age, like this very boy.

From behind him, the hooded cultists started running from the pews. Newly released civilians shouted and retreated for the weapons and tool sheds in back. Baelin could not hear any of it, for his trance was too deep. It was a poor time for a lapse. A custom-made grenade bounced near Baelin's foot and spun in place beside the cell door. When a soldier's cry finally sounded in his ears, he dove into the chamber and protected the shocked child from the looming blast.

The grenade detonated and shook the cavern, killing two women and wounding one soldier. Baelin's ears rang from the explosion, but the child was safe. Because he was in shock, the boy looked into the paladin's eyes and tried to believe that what he saw was real. The able soldiers and civilians alike took arms and met the oncoming reaper legion in desperate combat. While inside the cell, a brawny reaper snatched Baelin out and flung him into the back of the nearest pew.

As the battle raged on about them, Baelin could not help but gawk up at the sight of the giant. Portraying Goliath himself, this Blood Reaper was bald with a thick beard and an extraordinary muscular frame. He grunted with a haughty smile and moved in to finish off the weakened paladin. Baelin evaded the first crushing pound of the beast and, in seconds, executed another narrow escape. He waited for one more attack so that he could implement a suitable counter strike worthy enough to put the ogre down for good.

Instead, the battle became a one-sided thrashing. Baelin suffered nearly every blow. One strike sent the Divine Mace flying out of his hands and into the obscurity of the turmoil. Baelin fell to his knees and spit out blood, debating whether he had any internal injuries. The brute returned while cracking his knuckles. Baelin, however, was willing to kneel only to God.

Lifting up his head, he caught the reaper in the chin by surprise and proceeded to deliver fierce punches, elbows, and knees into his enemy. The flurry of strikes upset the beast, but that was all. The reaper clouted Baelin in the left side of the face and then offered a stern hook into his right side. Blood spewed out from his face like the first lash of a soaked towel.

The paladin refused to give in to his adversary, landing some hits, though receiving the worst of the fight. A final punch to the head reopened the gash on his face. He wondered how much more he could stand. The brute kneed him into the stomach, picked him up over his shoulder, and threw him into the weapon shed. Baelin crashed through the half-opened door and rolled onto the floor, groaning in pain. In spite of this, a small glimmer of hope looked him right in the eye — the Divine Mace.

When the reaper entered the shed to end the fight on his terms, there was a small trace of blood on the ground and nothing else. From the top ledge of the busy shed, Baelin shouted like a warrior and came down with the full might of his mace. The telling strike cracked open the back of the brute's head, killing him before hitting the ground. Looking at the thug's bleeding carcass, he knew that it was he who knocked him out three years back in Swamp Hill. The intensity of the blows confirmed the identity of his long-lost nemesis. He was sure of it.

Any who witnessed Baelin fall into the weapon shed with the reaper champion to follow discerned that the paladin was finished. For two reapers who approached the shed with grins, they learned that assuming was dangerous. After a loud exertive shout, a spear soared out from the darkness of the shack and skewered one of them through the chest. Others who saw this omitted their previous rival and tended to the curious happening.

Onlookers watched a maimed Arl Baelin march out of the shed wielding his mace, a steel shield emblazoned with a phoenix, and a demeanor that terrified even his allies. His hair dripped with blood and sweat, only proving that he was still alive. Pain had become an afterthought. A slam with the shield and a strike from the mace mowed down any challengers in three moves or less. Baelin's vigor was matchless in combat, inspired by the fate of his wife and child.

The brawl became instinctual for him. Cursing and shouting like a feral animal, Baelin flouted any hurt and fought on. His world became slow and dizzy with every next victory. Soon enough, the ground became red with blood and the reapers were lessening in numbers, startled that they were waning. Along with two soldiers, many civilians had died valiantly in the hostility. Seeing this brought Baelin to tears. He had to stay awake and save as many captives as his body would allow.

As he battled on, a voice resonated in his mind, saying, "*Fear not, soldier of the Lord, for your lungs are filled with the breaths of angels. Your heart shall beat more blood than you spill this night. The wicked shall become your footstools.*"

Before he could comprehend whether the serene voice was celestial or not, Samuel ran over to him and shouted, "You will not make it any longer down here! You must escape while you can still take care of yourself!"

Jaded, Baelin replied, "I cannot leave. Too many have died!"

"Up that path there!" Samuel grasped his shoulder and pointed towards the northern passageway, "That will lead you out! As long as you feel an incline, you will know that you are going the right way! Do not turn back!"

"And what of you?" Baelin shook his head to awaken his senses, "You can't defeat them all!"

Samuel cried as he rejoined the battle, "We are trapped down here if you don't find a way to the surface in time! Go!"

Dropping the burdening shield, Baelin ran into the weapon shed guarded by two armed civilians and put two grenades into his pouch for desperate measures. He raced up the northern tunnel and never looked back, praying that Samuel and the remaining fighters could hold their own against the Blood Reapers. On his run, Baelin encountered two escaped prisoners who helped him. Together, they scurried up the incline with all of their strength.

Reaching a checkpoint, three other escapees knelt behind a small barricade and hushed them. Now, the six of them hid behind the obstruction and mulled over the latest setback. A group of eight reapers stood watch over the egress with weapons drawn. They knew about the fighting inside, but rebuffed any concern about joining the tussle. The fiends felt it better to remain at the exit and strike down any pathetic captives who tried for a daring escape.

These cannibal cowards did not count on the paladin. Baelin quietly emptied his satchel and offered the pair of grenades to any who thirsted for vengeance. Two volunteers gladly took the shells and calculated their tosses. Simultaneously, the escapees hurled the grenades for the last obstacle and listened to the reapers holler in dismay. The two of a kind detonated together, making for a deafening discharge. None of the reapers were safe from the blast, as debris and smoke filled the tunnel.

The frenzied escapees charged the stunned throng of cultists and finished off any survivors. As one, they ran for the exit and lifted the final door out like a sewer cover. The night sky revealed a gorgeous network of stars, reveling in their escape. It seemed so beautiful. Fresh air filled their lungs as they ran out into the field one by one. Some of them were captives for a week, while others suffered for longer. Yet now, thanks to Islandia's paladin, they were free.

One of them was able to judge their location from the stars above and proposed that they all head to the east for Bayport. Baelin, on the other hand, found his own marker. The Midvein Mansion was but three hundred yards up the road. All along, the trap door into the tunnels hid in the dead grass just off the road to

Chimera. For the first time, he looked upon the site with gratefulness rather than dread.

"Paladin, will you come with us?" One of them whispered.

Baelin could hardly acknowledge their sentiments, for his mind, body, and soul strived to reach the mansion. Still gripping the Divine Mace with force, he dispersed from the group and vanished from their sight. Was Gideon still waiting for him? Did she leave and fend for herself? Did Cainam find her alone and helpless? Baelin spew forth more blood as he ran, worrying on the worst-case scenarios.

Passing the dead bodies he left in front of the mansion, he bustled into the dilapidated sanctuary and headed for the master bedroom. Scaling the stairs in a stupor, Baelin heard the heavenly voices enter his head, *"Like a lamp in the darkness, the righteous dispels all evil. Here you shall find rest and rise as the North Star, attracting others to you. They will come to your aid."*

He collapsed on the stairway, feeling his blood drain from untended wounds. Again, he tried to climb the staircase. The Divine Mace had become a burden, though he would not let it go. When he felt as if he would not make it, Gideon reached out her hands and pulled him up the final three steps. Seeing how injured he was, she helped him into the master bedroom and placed him onto the mattress, fearful of his dire condition.

With her wounds healed well enough, Gideon tore off parts of her attire and formed various tourniquets around his body. He was weak and going into shock from heavy exertion and blood loss. Lethargic, Baelin tried to speak to her, but his adrenalin had peaked. From living off the land for so many years of her life, Gideon was proficient in emergency treatment for someone at this critical stage. Emotions from the pit of her soul started to release while helping him.

She whimpered with concern, "Arl, stay with me. You are going to be alright. You are with me now. I will watch over you."

Baelin turned his head to see her worried face and smiled, declaring drowsily, "I still love you."

Whether he was enervated or lucid, Gideon believed him. She wanted to break free from the anger, grief, and guilt that imprisoned her for three years, but was unsure how to do it. The fear of evoking the past was too great for her now. Gideon, as strong and imprudent as she was, did not know what to say. Baelin still had a part of her heart and he was not going to let go of it.

Before she could utter a word, a resonation of Cainam's voice filled the mansion, "**You fools. Why do you insist on living when there is no hope left? I could have crushed your skulls with my one hand any time I liked. I alone am your hope and your despair.**

"**Do you think you have done something this night? You believe that you have made a difference in my devices? You will live just long enough to learn that you live only because I allow it. Thus, as a sentence for defying me, you will burn! At last, you will burn!**"

Baelin clenched his fists in anger of hearing his sinister voice, but Gideon sensed his very presence. She ran out onto the veranda and peered out into the night. There, she beheld a small army of Blood Reapers head for the mansion with torches, screaming and laughing. Her nerves rattled at the sight. Youths and adults all carried the flame, seeking to burn the useless manor to the ground.

She ran back inside and shouted, "They're going to set the place on fire!"

Each reaper had their turn of casting the torch. They hurled the fires into the windows and onto the balconies. Some slipped inside and put aflame specific rooms or stairways. The Midvein Mansion withstood the centuries. It survived harsh weather and a changing atmosphere. While some believed that the spirits within kept it alive, there was no vindication for its fate now. With the house cleansed of all dark power, Kirk Cainam and his reapers had no more use for it. The great manor, like man, would turn to ash and dust.

Smoke quickly rose to the highest floors and some flames lit up the night sky. Already, parts of the house began to fall apart. The dry wood lit up like fig leaves in a bonfire, leading to the mansion's ultimate collapse in due time. Gideon, the great sorceress, felt hopeless. All the magic in her arsenal was no match for the fast acts of the hungry flame. Baelin rolled out of bed and onto the floor, compelling her to come to his aid.

"Leave me here! There is still time for you to escape! Go!" He cried from the ground.

"No! I won't do that!" She shouted back as the smoke began to fill the level, "How much can that mace of yours do?"

"Not miracles." He chuckled in the realization of his fate.

After looking at her fair face, Baelin glanced out at the smoky night. He took one last look at his homeland, feeling Gideon hold him in her nursing arms. Yet, the sound of the Islandic horn suddenly boomed and devoured the revolting cries of the reapers. As his world went black from the smoke, he could feel her pull his arm and drag his limp body along the floor. The cries of battle echoed outside and he finally lost consciousness. In the end, there was no more pain. There was no more worry — only silence, peace, and rest.

Redeem the Knight
Faith IX

One month ago...

For those who were fortunate enough to catch a glimpse of Islandia's paladin, they rarely ever saw him without his canine companion. They traversed the island together, Arl and Alec, as the best of friends. No journey was too long and no adventure was too short, for the years of bitter loneliness were behind them. As most nights, they sat about the fire within their isolated basilica sanctuary and ate.

The holy knight and loyal dog shared a genuine trust that so many craved for, though never found. Arl poured his love into this dog as he would his son. God knew what kind of turmoil the hound had endured in the past, for Arl could read it in his eyes. Alec would lift his head and ears at the slightest hint of danger. Their care for each other was not unlike the love conveyed between best friends from school or childhood.

Poking lumber deeper into the flame, Arl said, "You know, Alec, life is not short. Life is damn long. It is our memory that is short. How can we be expected to recall every blessing and curse of every day? We let it all pass us by, selecting flashes of memoirs that define us. Perhaps it is time for us to make some new memories — better ones?"

Alec inquisitively lifted his head while his comrade proceeded, "God will set us free from this. He shall recognize the sincerity of our prayers and redeem us both. Do you believe me?"

When Alec lowered his head and whined, Arl patted between his ears and said, "Well, you should. Trade fear for faith, as I once said. 'It starts with belief and ends in relief.' Corny, I know, but it is true. My mother used to tell me that when I was a kid. Of all the hell we have experienced, Alec, hope is all that we have left. What else do we have? Nothing."

Arl stared into the crackling fire, entranced, as Alec rose onto his four paws in worry. He panted as a stewed canine would, tilting his head and observing his friend's stupor. Alec growled in an attempt to waken him. Arl snapped out of his musing and grinned, saying with gravity, "If hell breaks loose and I am in the middle of it, you cannot come with me. You are returning to Ron and that is it. No exceptions."

After Alec looked up at him in fear of being separated, Arl asked calmly, "Would you come back to me, boy? Would you try and find me?"

Alec barked happily and put his head onto Arl's lap, still looking up at him. The woof was reassuring. Even though he was just a dog, Alec was a true companion. He was a mix of the old world's German Shepard and the present world's natural selection. Arl, on the other hand, was the only paladin in Islandia now, when there used to be more. After his blasphemous deeds, the New Vatican found it counterproductive to station other holy knights on the lone island.

Even to the pope, it seemed like a punishment. Islandia was not a province that the Ellium Empire put much stake in. But for Arl and his dog, it was home. As the fire died out, Islandia's paladin fell asleep under the heavens and vigorously anticipated God's promise of redemption. Alec, on the other hand, licked his companion's hand before finding a cozy place to drift off.

Now, one month later...

Baelin could feel something lick his hand, emerging from nothingness. Almost immediately, the pain began to set in. The slightest movement presented him with a waking agony, particularly coming from spots swathed in bandages. From inside an individualized medical tent, he turned his head to make sure that it was actually Alec osculating with his hand and not just a common hound – or worse. His vision was blurred and his brain spun in the process.

However, there was his dog, panting with excitement while observing his companion come to. Baelin could hardly believe his eyes, for he left his dog with Ronald back in Linden. Clearly, he did not die in Midvein Mansion's fire. Yet, he could not place where he was now. His mind had not caught up to the present circumstances. Again, his wounds throbbed as his bandages held tight. The aching reminded him that he was not dreaming.

Before he could appreciate his current condition, Baelin heard a man's voice from somewhere inside the tent, "Let the captain know that the paladin is awake. Go on!"

Alec barked and, like a flash, a band of soldiers helped Baelin to sit up on his lanky bed. The medic gave him clean water to drink and tested his senses. Still in awe over the appearance of his dog, Baelin checked his bandages. He found that his face was stitched up along with his lower back and side. By way of a mirror, he peered into his beat eyes, one of them red from blood.

From the sounds of salute outside, Baelin anticipated the attention of an Islandic captain. Their armor was red and black, like the Special Forces unit that found him in the sanctuary days ago. In came the captain wielding the Divine Mace, wrapped in cloth. He placed it delicately on the medical table and approached the paladin respectfully.

Holding out his hand, the captain said, "I am Captain River Castle and this is my legion, the Rising Sirens. It is good to see you alive, paladin. God surely smiles upon you and those in your fine company."

Baelin attempted to respond, but he only incited a coughing fit. In the meantime, Captain Castle gestured for his men to leave them alone. He then pulled a small table over and set two seats. Checking the stiches on his face with his hand, Baelin muttered, "You found my dog."

As they both admired the behaved mutt, the captain sat in one of the chairs and said, "Actually, your dog found you. He entered our encampment this morning and tried to sneak into your tent here. My men shooed him away for a while, but it became clear that there was no stopping him. We let him in to see you and, well, here he is."

Against all odds, his dog had fulfilled an unwritten promise in finding him. Baelin pushed himself off his bed and petted his trusty companion, forcing a kneel to meet him on the same eye level. Alec licked his face and whimpered at the sight of him. The captain rubbed his eyes before looking over the paladin much closer. This marked the first time he had ever spoken to the controversial avenger. He seemed more like a living legend than a disgraced knight of the holy order.

"How do you feel?" Captain Castle thought it was a stupid question, but could not think of anything else to say.

"Like I look." Baelin rose to his feet and retorted, paying attention to his obliging company.

The captain nodded with affinity and waited for the paladin to sit across from him at the square table. When Baelin pulled out the chair and sat down, grunting all the way, the wounded warrior asked, "How long have I been out?"

"Two and a half days." Castle finally answered, despite Baelin's stunned gaze, "You were beaten real bad when we found you. It's a miracle that you survived at all, to put it plainly."

Taken aback, he then asked the captain, "How exactly did you find me?"

Castle replied, "Well, when you light up a big haunted mansion in the dead of night, it attracts attention."

Baelin said without much deliberation, "Fair enough."

"We camped a little further west from Bayport than Spire and Dolan told you." The captain continued, "There was something suspicious about this sudden mission, as you probably sensed yourself, so we helped ourselves to some reconnaissance. One of my scouts spotted the blazing house first. Then, Lieutenant Dolan ran into a few emaciated escape artists. They told us about what was going on down there and the rest is bloody history."

Tuning out the pain, Baelin confessed, "I was dead."

"Almost." Castle interjected, "We ambushed the Blood Reapers and routed them in minutes. As for you, that mace fell from the balcony and almost hit me. One of my boys, Karlus Rite, you'll meet him later, scaled the wall and found you up there out cold. It was not long after that the mansion started coming down. Sergeant Rite is a big boy. Any more time and you would have been a pile of holy ash."

Taking it all in, Baelin shook his head and declared, "I don't know how to thank you. I am in your debt."

The captain sighed before saying, "Bullshit. I did not tell you the rest. Because of you, we discovered the truth behind that drifter village. A Blood Reaper haven. To be honest, paladin, I have not the slightest idea how you did it. Seventy-eight. We found a total of seventy-eight slain reapers inside that place. It was the damndest thing I ever saw.

"You saved many innocent lives that night. Out of the four missing soldiers, three of them survived the ordeal. Hell, we recovered stolen properties and uncovered a plot to assassinate over thirty officials, including that of the governor and every mayor of every city in Islandia. Whatever they were planning down there, it was big. It was epic."

"And the child?" He bore the small boy in his heart.

"Alive." Castle said, watching the paladin bow his head in relief, "Naturally, some other poor bastards didn't make it. They held their own in that pothole. We have a few reapers in custody. The others bit their tongues and bled to death. If we learned anything from this, it's that this cult just will not go away."

Staring blindly into the table, Baelin said somberly, "May God save us all."

As they sat amid a brief silence, a soldier entered the tent and whispered in his captain's ear. When the soldier left, Castle patted the table and stood up, saying reverently, "I wanted to tell you this myself. The documents you uncovered in those tunnels have been sent to Emperor Eli Ellis IV. He shall know of your victory."

"You honor me." Baelin said, while petting his dog. Thinking of his lost son, Alec, he recalled what Gideon had done to preserve his life in the mansion. There was still a hint of care in her. There was a small sentiment of love lost somewhere in her bitter heart. If only their son was still alive. Only that would awaken her from the nightmare world she chose for herself.

He asked before Castle could speak, "Captain, did your men find a woman up there with me?"

Curious, the captain replied, "Only you, paladin. Were you not alone?"

"No." Baelin said, recalling the voices in his head, "Angels were with me."

Finding that the progressing dialogue had reached its course, Captain Castle began to head for the camp, saying, "If you will have him, paladin, you have a visitor."

"To be true, captain, I would much rather be alone." Baelin spoke jadedly.

"You will want to see this visitor. Believe me." Captain Castle offered a fleeting salute before exiting the medic's tent.

Baelin shook his head and sighed. For all that he had done to cleanse Midvein Mansion, it was the Blood Reapers that propelled him to higher ground. Still, he could not understand why Kirik Cainam did not kill him. And what of Gideon? Did she survive the fire? His head hurt from the swirling events and questions without anyone to answer them. In the meantime, his precious friend sat by his side and wagged his tail. He, at least, offered a comforting reminder of what companionship felt like.

While mulling over his present circumstances, Baelin lifted his head to offer an obligatory greeting to his next visitor. In contrast, a revered figure of his past entered the medical tent in full regalia. He stood lofty, though humble. Seemingly wise beyond his years, Magistrate Mason himself bowed his head to his fellow paladin and took a moment to assess his condition.

Mason ogled his acolyte and pronounced with concern, "Arl, thank God you are alive!"

Baelin could hardly believe what he was seeing. All that he could muster was, "Mason?"

As the honored paladin neared closer, Baelin rose from his seat and embraced him. They hugged tightly, though his wounds would have preferred a simple handshake. It had been three years since they had set eyes on each other. Even then, it was not under good conditions. Together, they took to their seats and reveled in the light of their company.

"Are you hungry—thirsty?" Mason asked as Baelin sat down after him.

Practically disregarding the question, Baelin asked in wonder, "What are you doing here? How did you—"

"That will be answered soon." Mason interceded, "I have come to ensure your safety. I feared that he would have gotten to you before I could. After all, you survived him and his snakes."

At last, he remembered the connection between the supreme leader of the reapers and his childhood. Baelin's beam dissipated as he said grimly, "You knew, Mason. You knew about Cainam and his scheme to lure me into his hands."

Regretfully, Mason lowered his head and, after a moment of silence, replied, "I had a suspicion that he would try to ensnare you, but never knew how or when. Upon receiving the dossier to this wretched mansion, it all seemed too curious, but I had to be sure. Truly, Arl, I am sorry."

"Why didn't you tell me?" Baelin riposted, "For all of my life as a paladin here, I was endangered by this lunatic. All this time, I rid the island of a puppet leader. As I suffered the loss of my family and rank in the holy order, he plotted against me. You told me that he suffered 'a fate worse than death.' I disagree."

Mason stroked his beard frantically before readjusting his posture, saying with solemnity, "Arl, what I am about to tell you is known only by the High Magistrates and Pope David. Not even the emperor himself knows of this. I, myself, only came upon this knowledge about four years ago. This must stay between us, do you understand?"

As Baelin prudently nodded his head, Mason proceeded, "You know of the beginnings of Ellium? The first Ellis ousted Vestilus, the sorcerer king, and assumed the throne for himself? Ellis sent an able band of paladins to hunt the sorcerer down and kill him. Fifteen holy knights set out to slay Vestilus at Mount Gambit in the northwest. As the story goes, Vestilus put up a fight, but was eventually defeated by the paladins. This is not true. They were picked off by the evil sorcerer, one knight every day, until only five remained.

"In the end, four turned back in fear that they would not survive the harsh hoary climate of the mountains. One paladin stood up to this exiled sorcerer king. The paladin ultimately defeated him, but with horrifying consequences. He still had to deliver the carcass back to King Ellis as evidence of the deed. This is where the story takes a blasphemous turn.

"The winter was unforgiving high upon Mount Gambit and the forlorn knight was hungry and without food. In his thirst for life, he ate what was on hand. Resorting to cannibalism, he ate the corrupted flesh of Vestilus. This profane act of desperation has set in motion a grave twist of circumstances."

"Are you saying that Kirik Cainam is a descendant of this doomed paladin?" Baelin asked from behind his bandages.

Somber, Mason said, "I am saying that he *is* Kirik Cainam."

Even Alec failed to utter a sound. The hairs on the nape of Baelin's neck stood up as he desperately tried to fathom Mason's daunting tale. He blurted out in his confusion, "But that was over a hundred years ago!"

"Yes, it was." Mason fostered Baelin's fear, saying further, "Cainam's aging has slowed down significantly, if not stopped all together. He has absorbed Vestilus's wicked power in blood. For that reason, the blood of his victims sustains him now, keeping him young. Have no doubt, he has gained great influence in his seclusion. His powers have increased and he has learned much about what he is capable of doing."

Still stunned by the saga, Baelin stammered in his dismay, "How can this be? How long did the New Vatican know of this?"

Mason took a deep breath before saying, "It was not until he returned home that we learned of Cainam's true identity. Arl, the house you grew up in was the house that Kirik Cainam built and lived in with his own family before leaving for Mount Gambit. That was why he chose your family's household. It was all his at one point. You see, you are what he could have been if he remained in Linden.

"In a sense, he wants to destroy you, because you have become what he could not be. Cainam will not be hasty in killing you, either. He knows that you cannot leave the island. His ultimate wish is to make you suffer, to taint you and everything you ever loved. When we chased him from your home that fateful day, not even I knew that he was the rogue paladin of that notorious fable. Soon after, he just vanished. He was gone."

"God redeem us." Baelin groaned, "He had a chance to kill me. It was the perfect opportunity to take his vengeance."

"The Midvein Mansion fire proves that he can be pushed to impulsivity." Mason considered his pupil's awful condition and went on in a softer tone, "That is why we must partake in his game of patience and provoke him. I am sure that you are not his main concern, Arl. His aspirations lie in Ellium and, perhaps, the known world. I have studied him—"

"Please, no more." Baelin held his aching head, and opened with a sorrowful passion, "All that I ever wanted was to please the Lord. In keeping watch of Islandia, I was a true paladin—a holy knight worthy of the mace. Even you had said that I was on course for making elite rank. I wore the Armor of God, nearly every day, knowing that I was chosen to protect and defend the people. My family was proud.

"I was happy once, Mason. Now, look at me! Take a good look now that you can! Was has become of me? The sanctum branded my wife and child as unholy, pitiful perversions of the church! That was my family! If they were able to forsaken all of us to the shadow will of a fallen paladin with demonic powers, then I can raise any family I damned well choose!

"I tell you the truth, I am shattered! I am worn by this! I prayed to God every night for one chance to redeem myself and your signed order fell into my hands. You do not understand what that meant to me. I was alone with only a dog to accompany me! Upon receiving the mission to cleanse that miserable place, my heart was filled with hope.

"Instead, I am here in this tent, thrashed, learning that I could have been killed by a small army of Blood Reapers led by a supernatural rogue paladin hiding within the island without consequence for nearly all my life! I did not warrant this! I deserved more respect! I sacrificed my very life for you pompous magistrates and I will not be regarded as a heretic!"

Hearing Baelin's irrepressible outburst, the guards from outside peered into the tent in distress. Mason waved them off silently and permitted his fellow paladin to recover from his earned tirade. Alec leapt onto all fours and growled at the guards until they left. Baelin caught each painful breath and endured the throbbing of his wounds. His rant did not come without a price of fleeting agony.

"Forgive me, Mason." He said as he held his side, "I spoke out in anger."

"No, it is I that must ask for forgiveness." Mason clasped his hands as if to pray, "I was not there for you. Not only are you my paladin brother, but you are my friend. You are like a son to me. For my part in your suffering, I have come here to seek salvation. As of today, you will walk the path to redemption on your own no more. I will share this burden with you until you are free to return to your family in Ellium. That is my word."

Taken aback by his mentor's honorable words, Baelin replied, "But you are a magistrate now. How can you – "

Mason interrupted, "Not any more. I resigned a week after signing the order that led you to near ruin. My full rank as Legion Leader of Islandia has been reinstated. As we were once, we shall be again. This time, I will pursue Cainam and end his tale."

It all seemed as if he was hallucinating. The sudden confession from his mentor found its mark at Baelin's heart. The greatest times of his life were spent at Mason's side. When Legion Leader Mason became Magistrate Mason, he was never replaced. The New Vatican regarded Islandia as a province unfit for holy expansion, so Baelin became the only paladin. Legion leaders were pulled from the island and all eight of the holy knights returned to Ellium. Arl Baelin became the lone paladin.

Astounded by Mason's admission, Baelin spluttered, "I do not know what to say. Why did you resign? What did they say?"

"The Lord traps the wise in their own ruses." Mason said, "I am not a judge or an elder. My place is here, where my best years were with me. I have my mace and armor again. The helmet still fits. How can I live with myself if I renounce my true calling? Whether it was vengeance or apathy, we shall find redemption for our sins together."

With Alec panting by his side, Baelin rose from the rickety chair and clasped Mason's wrist, saying, "For any transgressions you believe you have against me, know that they are forgiven."

An honorable embrace turned compassionate as the two knights hugged each other, finding mercy in their company. Their eyes moistened as they let go of their burdens for a moment. It felt good to cry and drop their guard without fear of compromising repute. Alec whimpered at the sight and pawed Baelin's leg, a gull for heartfelt moments.

After a stern pat on the arm, Mason said to him, "Fresh air would do you good, boy. Do you feel well enough for a walk?"

"I have slept long enough." Baelin replied, using the staff to his right to balance himself.

And so, Mason, Baelin, and Alec emerged from the tent to witness an endearing spectacle. Soldiers and civilians alike congregated about the campsite to admire Baelin's resolve. As he looked upon the growing crowd, gradual claps began to form. Like an onrushing storm, the welcoming mass began to applaud in his honor. Baelin limped deeper into the encampment, surrounded by a standing ovation, and humbly smiled in gratitude.

The prolonged applause came from everyone, especially the survivors of the reapers' internment. While still scrawny, they praised his heroic actions in their daring rescue and subsequent escape. From the adoring crowd, a young boy raced over and hugged him at the waist. Baelin received the child and cleared his throat, attempting to avoid crying a second time. When Samuel came up next, he embraced him with honor and nodded his head, taking in every redeeming moment.

Paladins were taught to accept their rewards in heaven. This day, however, served as remedy, rather than reward. His heart had bled for years, alone and forsaken. Somehow, a horrifying trial bred a hopeful phenomenon. The cruel entrapping set him on higher ground, aided by characters on the worldly and celestial plane. But, in the end, it took the will of a noble soul and feisty spirit to rise from the ashes of despair.

The freed boy pet Alec's thick coat, enthralled by the canine's joyful disposition. Mason beheld the whole scene from outside the pooling throng as Baelin met his fellow Islandic compatriots. Under better conditions, they eagerly greeted the remarkable paladin and gave him reverence. He rekindled his faith. He renewed his devotion to God and His people. With conviction that his beloved son, Alec, blessed him from above, Baelin would be steadfast in his calling.

Though he would never tell anyone, he knew that Gideon somehow saved his life. No one could uncover this, for her identity as the Witch of Swamp Hill would be revealed. As his new friends congregated around him, Baelin wondered what had happened to her after blacking out. He wanted to thank her for what she did. She had the chance to leave him when he had gone back to the village. If she did, he most certainly would have died.

Yet, from inside Swamp Hill's murky refuge, Gideon stood over the pond and gazed into its rippling forethoughts. There she watched Baelin recover from his grave injuries and accept the alms of gratefulness from those he saved. While her disciples stood behind her, she opened her hand and considered Baelin's blood ring. She stole it from the small pouch tied to his belt buckle. Serving as a memento, Gideon clenched the ring in her hand and let the images of Baelin drown in the undulations.

At the same time, Baelin reached into his little pouch to make certain that his blood ring was still there. Upon achieving redemption, he would be permitted, as he saw it, to put the ring back onto his ring finger. Instead, he found nothing there. The ring was gone. While he thought of many scenarios, only one made the most sense. Whether she took it as a keepsake or a device to experiment with, Gideon would have known that Baelin had all intentions of returning to retrieve it.

Therefore, another chapter had begun in Arl Baelin's story. This time, he was no longer alone for its telling. His name was now accompanied with the number seventy-eight. Survivors of the dreaded Blood Reapers' keep spoke of his name in high regard. Newly appointed Legion Leader Mason swore an oath to walk alongside his path in seeking the reclamation of their names.

Still controversial by many standards in Islandia and Ellium, Baelin's journey to redemption would not be easy. Kirik Cainam's whereabouts were unknown to the people, for most had never even heard of him. Until he defeated the fallen paladin and severed the link between them, Baelin could not be saved. Though the road seemed perilous and impossible, he was armed with a rejuvenated faith. It was this new faith that served as the only weapon strong enough to redeem the knight.

*Concept cover drawing by Hugo Bravo

Redeem the Knight
Epilogue X

The rain came and softened the ruins of Midvein Mansion, leaving it a rank graveyard of a prior age. Having stood for centuries by means no architect or archeologist could explain, it now, like Sarah, rested in peace. The new moon blackened the unnerving site and everything else ruined or burnt to ash. If only more had realized the significance of Midvein. It found only one sustainable suitor: Kirik Cainam.

The psychotic paladin of myth ambled about the remnants of a once great asylum for knowledge. Smoke still managed to rise up amidst the rain after days of its destruction. Cainam sighed as he rambled, searching for some relics of interest. He had read most of the literature from the library, even some of the medical journals. Yet, now, it was lost to the world. So many truths had burned to the heavens, never to fall upon the concentrations of humanity.

Nevertheless, Cainam trampled over a book of even greater consequence. The Compendium was charred and blackened, but still held great significance. In effect, the owners of the book were responsible for adding critical data into its pages concerning the titles of important leaders and their whereabouts, main centers of knowledge and prayer, and various secrets known only to the order. Cainam had not belonged to the order for some time and was in need of classified intelligence.

Though many pages were scorched beyond reading, some were still in tolerable shape. The Holy Bible somehow survived the fire, but he could care less about it. Cainam tossed it away and rummaged through the overcooked case, finding only a seared bedroll and other futile articles. Unearthing nothing else of use in the ruins of the mansion, he spit on the ground and skimmed through the delicate pages of the Compendium.

"Why did you not kill him, Kirik?" A voice stemmed from one of twelve red hooded minions standing about the front lawn, "All this preparation and timing for nothing?"

"Nothing, you say? Your ignorance disturbs me." Cainam replied ominously while scrolling the pages, "Do you believe I am no better than a thug, mindlessly bludgeoning my enemies without calculation or subterfuge? Arl Baelin has not escaped my grasp. His harlot witch and timely band of merry men rescued him from a burning building. That is all.

"He bested me in battle and overthrew Chimera. He exercised the mansion of any spirits and left it a futile shell of shit. Let it return to ash. Let the knowledge of thousands of years become buried by its miserable end, for I have foreseen the fate of the world. I shall usher it in. Do you expect a simple paladin with a curfew to stop me?

"You give him too much. Arl Baelin shall meet his end by my hands, as it was meant to be. I shall not slay him in vain. No, he will die alone and empty without his wench to save him. After his bones bleach in the sun, his family will share the same doom. You are bemused by my composure, as anyone else would be. That is because you are blind and can see only what is right in front of your dumfounded face."

The red hooded minion holding a small child by the hand spoke out, saying, "You turned him into a hero."

Kirik Cainam closed the marred book with his one hand before nearing closer to them, "So you think. I admit that I underestimated his will, but that, too, has passed. Our next confrontation shall not deliver such regrettable results."

Kneeling before the young trembling boy, he continued, "You are so anxious that you fail to see the key to our advantage."

"If Arl Baelin finds—" Another minion cautiously warned, "When Arl Baelin discovers that we have his only son, he will come for us with an unrelenting wrath. Don't you see that?"

Upon stroking Alec's fair chin with his finger, Kirik Cainam smiled and said, "See it? I am counting on it."

Amongst the aftermath of Midvein Mansion's demise, the mysteriously hooded members of the Blood Reapers mounted on their horses and rode off to their secret positions scattered all about Islandia. They were of the last reaper elites under Cainam's power. He observed them gallop away in different directions. The one in custody of the boy headed east to Babylonia, as per their leader's instructions. When they were all out of the spying eyes of lingering scouts, Cainam pulled over his hood and skimmed through the readable pages of the Compendium.

By either fate or celestial design, his eyes fell upon the edict:

82. As the serpent must crawl in dirt, so shall the deserter of righteousness. Upon rain from the heavens, they shall drown. From the dust of the desert, they shall choke. By the boot of the just, they will squirm. Let it be known, that the serpent cannot find safety in its burrows. If the holy order does not flush them out, the Most High God shall make it a tomb.

$\overset{\text{v}}{\Omega}$

www.ingramcontent.com/pod-product-compliance
Lightning Source LLC
Chambersburg PA
CBHW051834170626
46807CB00003B/1167